Layout by K. Allen Wood
Cover artwork by Frank Walls
Black T-Shirt Books logo by Chris Enterline

www.adamcesare.com

Printed in the United States of America.

ZERO
LIVES REMAINING
ADAM CESARE

Art!
Game Pr!

New York • Pennsylvania

To my love, Jen.

*Also, to my friend Scott and anyone else who's
helped make Philly my new home.*

And to you, for reading this.

PROLOGUE

In the minutes before the horrific accident that would end his unspectacular life, Robby Asaro was engaged in one of his favorite activities. He was making a pizza.

The frozen dough arrived shrink-wrapped, looking like a big pale Frisbee. There were twenty to a case, ten in each stack, packed double-wide and weighing about fifty pounds. Inside the plastic wrap was a pre-portioned bag of cheese and another of sauce.

To aid in pizza-preparation, a set of instructions came stapled to the inside of every lid. Robby went through the boxes and tossed the directions in the trash before loading the pizzas into the walk-in cooler.

The company wanted to make you think prep was idiot-proof, but there was still an art to making a Funcave pizza edible, something that you couldn't be told via step-by-step instructions.

Robby Asaro went beyond making them edible: he had elevated these pizzas to an art.

He liked to tell people that it was his Italian heritage, his grandmother's kitchen voodoo filtering down through the bloodline, but it was really just a decade of trial and error.

Robby had been in the pizza-thawing business since 1980, a year after Funcave had opened its doors. Over the last decade he'd learned nothing about women through a marriage and a divorce, but at least he'd learned when to ignore the instructions and when to trust the oven.

Eddie Harmon, the owner of Funcave and Robby's boss, liked

to describe the oven as "automated" but Robby had never seen Mr. Harmon try to work the thing.

The appliance was big enough that it took up half the kitchen. A piece of machinery that huge was never simple.

Robby washed his hands, toweled off, and then dusted his palms with a bit of flour while still damp. He set aside the sauce and cheese and gave the dough a layer of flour, too. The instructions didn't call for flour. That was all Robby.

The tomato sauce was best applied with a spoon, the contours of the utensil allowing for organic peaks and valleys in sauce distribution. Robby only used three-quarters of a bag, any more than that and you'd have a soggy pizza.

Robby sprinkled the cheese, tossing in a bit of parmesan powder for flavor. That didn't come in the box, he had to order it separately and bill it as something else so Eddie wouldn't catch him. Paying more for the pizzas than the owner deemed necessary was a one-way ticket to a patented Mr. Harmon chew-out.

The oven was built like a long conveyor belt. It looked like it would be more at home in a quarry, rocks and sand moving across it, than a video arcade. But here it was.

The belt's tread was made of a fine metal grating that moved the pizza under the heating coils. The metal of the tread itself heated up, giving each pizza a crispy bottom during its trip through the oven. By the end of a rotation, the grating was well over four hundred degrees.

Simple, the machine wasn't. There were separate settings for each of the three heating coils, the speed of the belt, and the coils could even be lowered closer to the track.

After years of tinkering, Robby had the oven just the way he liked it, but that didn't stop the day-shift assholes from tampering with it.

From outside the kitchen, the sounds of the arcade floor entered through the order window. Robby put the finishing touches on the pizza while listening to the constant clatter of skeeballs being dropped into their troughs. When there was a lull in the radio, from farther away Robby could hear the electronic beeps and simplistic music of *Galaga '88* and *Spy Hunter.*

Robby Asaro smiled to himself, content with his place in life, feeling at one with the Zen of the arcade. He lifted up the cold dough with two hands until it was at eye-level. Dressed in sauce and cheese, it was a thing of beauty.

For most of his thirty-eight years, Robby had worked with his hands. Road crew, landscaping, even a brief stint as a field hand. None of those jobs were as tough on his mitts as prepping pizzas at the Funcave. The backs of Robby's hands were crisscrossed with scars, the patterns matching the cross-hatching of the conveyor belt.

Careful, this time, to keep his fingers away from the hot belt, he dropped the pizza on and watched as it started to slowly roll away, the hot orange glow of the heating coils stinging his eyes.

The assemblage of dough, sauce and cheese began its journey, by the time it reached its final station stop, it would no longer be an assemblage of distinct elements, but would instead be united as a pizza. A Funcave pizza.

"Hey, Rob," Seth yelled from the order window. Robby only half-listened to him, his eyes still fixed on the pizza as it inched down the conveyor belt, into the orange maw of the oven. "Now they say they want sausage and peppers on that. Don't throw it on yet."

It took him a moment to decode the words, and he was upset when he did.

Fucking kids, Robby thought. *Grow a pair, Seth. They should have to pay for two pizzas if they've already ordered.* That was what he thought, but he was not that kind of guy, so he shoved both hands into the conveyer belt to remove the pizza.

"Got it!" he yelled back.

Robby was two fingers deep into the rapidly-congealing dough. He gripped at the outer edges, the not-yet-crust of the pizza, and yanked it up from the metal grate. Amazingly, he had not burned himself, but he could feel the heat on his forearms through his chef's whites.

The last thought to cross Robby Asaro's mind that wasn't tinged with abject terror was how much he was going to sweat into his shirt and how he would have to do laundry later.

That was right before his sleeve snagged on the belt.

§

Seth rounded the corner of the kitchen doorway, responding to Robby's cries just in time to watch the older man's Reebok's disappear into the mouth of the oven. The sneakers made a sizzling sound with each crash against the metal grating, plastic vaporizing on contact.

Stepping inside the room, the smell of burning rubber mingled with burning hair so that it was impossible for Seth to tell which was which.

Or which was worse.

Located on a sparsely populated stretch of commercial road in Ashville, New Hampshire, Funcave was ten minutes from the closest EMT dispatch station. This is also about the same amount of time that it takes for a pizza to complete its roll through the oven.

By the time the paramedics arrived on the scene, most of Robby's clothes had burned away and his skin had taken on rosy hue. Even though the flesh was the color and texture of expertly prepared pepperoni, Robby Asaro was not around to appreciate it.

2014

CHAPTER 1

It was hard to concentrate on your game of *Ms. Pac-Man* when five feet away someone was calling you a "chink" under their breath.

Tiffany Park knuckled down, leaned into the machine and let her fist fuse with the joystick until plastic and flesh were indistinguishable.

The orange ghost was giving her trouble, had been the whole game. There was an unpredictability to *Ms. Pac-Man* that many classic games didn't possess. In this particular session, the orange ghost, Sue, was the embodiment of that randomness.

The decision to go for the warp tunnel proved fatal for Tiffany. Ms. Pac-Man spun onto her back in her death throes. It was less graphic than the death of Mr. Pac-Man—splitting at the middle and disappearing into himself—but not by much. The sight of Ms. Pac-Man on her ass, her ruby lips and beauty mark pointed to the sky, was beyond sad.

"No kill screen that time, Tiffany," Chris said, walking up behind her. "You would dishonor your family like that?" he added in a Mr. Miyagi accent.

Chris Murphy liked his metal nu and his stereotypes broad.

Tiffany had never achieved a kill screen in *Ms. Pac-Man*, not yet. Chris would never, but guys like Chris didn't care about shit like that.

Chris probably only knew the term kill screen because it included the word "kill" in it. The kid fit into the category of "hateful suburban white-boy" so snuggly that it may as well have been his race, ethnicity, and religion, too.

He took a step closer, reached a hand over so that he almost touched hers. She pulled her fingers back from the cabinet and he flicked the joystick.

"I've got next," he said. "Don't you see the token?"

There was no token, at least not pressed against the screen where it was supposed to be. It was pinched between two of Chris's dirty fingernails as he waved it in her face.

Chris was not fat or excessively tall, but he towered over Tiffany. He edged his way in front of the machine, the mass of his body pushing her out of the way without ever touching her, the mysterious force like the wrong end of a magnet.

From this close, Chris smelled like cigarette smoke and grease. At least she hoped it was cigarette smoke. Back in elementary school, Chris would boast to the other boys about spending his weekends torching stray cats.

"Let a man show you how it's done, China Girl."

It was hard for Tiffany to tell whether she was being bullied or hit on. There may have been some overlap between Chris's definitions of both terms.

Was she supposed to stay and watch him play *Ms. Pac-man*? The idea disgusted her. She looked down both ends of the aisle. They were alone. The classic gameroom wasn't very popular, so it was quite possible that they were the only two people on the second floor of Funcave.

From downstairs she could hear the infrequent crash of pins from the bowling alley. It was a Tuesday afternoon. The local kids only swamped the place on weekends and the old-timers that spent their nights trying to one-up each other's scores in *Tempest* and *Marble Madness* were not yet out of their minimum wage nine-to-fives.

Chris yanked the joystick. His wasn't the tight, professional grip that Tiffany tried to maintain, but the insane throttle of a man trying to break Ms. Pac-Man into submission.

The grip wouldn't work for the later levels, was real amateur-hour stuff, but he was competent enough to get through the first two stages without dying. He missed the first set of cherries, though.

Violent as his play-style was, fixating on the game, his strategy, was enough to quiet Tiffany's original fears about being alone with the Murphy boy. It was possible that he was one of those bullies whose rage stemmed from a desire to be befriended, so maybe this was his way of reaching out to someone, anyone.

Ms. Pac-Man found herself boxed into a corner without a power pellet and the ghosts descended upon her.

"Fuck! Stupid whore didn't go left." Chris screamed and Tiffany felt angry at herself for trying to humanize him. The circumstances didn't much matter: Chris Murphy was ugly, inside and out.

"There was a wall there." Tiffany said.

"Don't you think I know that? I wasn't yelling at you, was I? I'm mad at myself more than anything. We can't all be naturals. Americans don't come hardwired for this shit, not like the Japanese."

"Korean."

"What?" Chris said, onto his second life, going back to the top corner with no power pellet, getting ready to repeat his mistake.

"I'm Korean, not Japanese, and you should head through the tunnel."

"Don't backseat drive! We both know how good you people are at driving." He dropped the insult too quickly, wasn't that quick-witted, it was apparent that he'd been saving that gem in his back pocket for when she gave him advice.

"Okay, fuck this," Tiffany said. She bent to pick up her purse from under the machine, intending to grab it and walk away. Chris moved his boot so it pressed down on both straps, pinning the bag to the floor.

"Hey, while you're down there." He thrust forward with his crotch, almost hitting her in the head with his knee.

"Move your foot, Chris!" She stood to look him in the eye, but his gaze was fixed on the game. He was still slamming the joystick, but at least now he was going in the right direction.

"You know my name, that's good," he said. They'd gone to the same elementary school and their high school class of 2015 had less than sixty kids in it. *Not* knowing his name would have been more impressive.

"Just stay and help me with this game," he said. "Then I'll go."

Chris Murphy was the worst at making friends. When she realized this, Tiffany felt encouraged by the knowledge that she would never hold this dubious title. She was second-worst material, tops.

"You're doing okay, but you need to make sure that you get the fruit in every level, too. That way if you have enough points later in the game, you'll have lives to spare. Everything from the peach onward is a must-get."

"You've really thought about this. That's weird."

"That's the game, if you want to be any good at it, you've got to know it a little."

He didn't respond well to her lessons, but he also wasn't raging against the machine anymore. Ms. Pac-Man ate it again and he changed the subject. "I'm more of a *Call of Duty* guy, myself."

She didn't want to point out that that was blazingly apparent. He had one more life yet and she still needed her purse back.

"Okay last life," she said. *Please make it a good one, I don't need you raging out and giving me a wedgie or swirly or some shit*, she thought.

He was six levels deep into the game and the ghosts were out of the box much faster now. All four were out on the field before he had even cleared a quarter of the dots.

"Don't waste a pellet when you can't eat all four ghosts. There." She touched the glass showing him where to turn and when to do it. He was pretty good when he had direction, clearing that stage while collecting most of the available points.

"Put your finger away, I can't see," he said and swatted her hand. His skin was damp and even paler than hers. The win had made him cocky, one level done correctly and now he was reverting back to his tough guy act.

Don't fuck up. Despite herself, she was now invested in this game, rooting for Chris Murphy, a desire beyond just wanting to get her purse back and run away from the large, creepy kid in the Slipknot sweatshirt.

Tiffany stared down at her Vans, too nervous to watch. Appraising herself, the fact that she was wearing her Bullet for my Valentine shirt, she realized something. To the other students in their senior class, she and Chris Murphy had probably belonged to the same breed of pissed-off mallrat, shared a genus. The thought depressed her.

When she glanced back up, Chris was dead, t he just didn't know it yet.

He'd eaten all the pellets and the ghosts were blinking back from blue. There was still about a third of the stage to clear of dots. Even a good player would have trouble with that, and Chris was mediocre.

Looking at the arrangement it was clear how he'd gotten so screwed so quickly. He was spooked by how fast his enemies were moving, running from corner to corner without trying to clear the dots, just stay alive.

"Uh oh," she said, and then wished she hadn't.

"Come on, you slut! Move!" Chris was back to his old self.

If this was what he yelled in public while trying to impress a girl, she tried to imagine what he yelled while he was playing *Call of Duty* with his friends. His online friends, the ones that didn't live in New Hampshire, had names like Smokemaster420.

"Calm down, it's just a game," Tiffany pleaded, seeing that the Game Over screen was seconds away.

Chris grunted something that could have sounded like slope, but maybe Tiffany's ears were too quick to hear slurs today.

Just as Ms. Pac-Man was about to slam into Sue (that damn pink bitch, again), a pixilated tremor passed over the screen and Ms. Pac-Man appeared on the opposite side of the ghost, unharmed.

"Whoa," Chris said. Childlike wonderment replacing his seething nerd-rage vitriol, "Did you see that?"

"Weird glitch."

"Glitch? Try mad skills, sugartits."

"Yeah, sure, great job." There was no skill involved. Ms. Pac-Man's magical teleportation had been a brain-fart of a thirty year old circuit board. She'd seen games wonk out at Funcave before.

It happened rarely, but it was nice when the glitches sometimes resulted at a second chance or extra life.

Chris finished up two more corners of the maze before finally being swallowed up by the gang of ghosts.

"Suck my dick you fruity rainbow ghosts!" Chris kept his hand on the joystick, used the leverage to propel his other fist forward into the Plexiglas of the cabinet. It didn't break, probably wouldn't if he'd had a sledgehammer instead of his doughy fist, but the joints of the cabinet did rattle.

"Can I have my bag now?" she asked.

Chris didn't move from the machine, but pressed his red knuckles to his cheek. It was clear that they'd be bruised tomorrow. Then he dipped his wounded hand down to his pocket and felt around.

"I'm all out of tokens. Give me one so I can play again. I think I'm getting a lot better."

She tossed him one, knowing that she was being shook down, but hoping beyond hope that he'd catch the coin, raise up his foot and let her get away from him.

Bending, she tugged on her purse.

He didn't lift his foot up.

"Let's go for one more. I need my sensei if I'm going to learn."

There was a loud popping sound like someone had stomped an inflated paper bag in the lunchroom.

Tiffany jumped, felt her veins flood with endorphins. She'd been coiled, on edge the whole time that Chris had been near her, ready to run and scream at any minute.

"Jesus," Chris yelled, pulling his hand away from the joystick. Tiffany smelled the stale locker-room stink of sweat and watched as a puff of smoke rolled out from between Chris's digits.

"What happened?"

"I think I was electrocuted."

Chris took a shaky step back from the machine and Tiffany snatched her purse from the carpeted floor. It didn't matter that he looked like he was about to puke or pass out, she was getting her bag before anything else.

"The handle's plastic." Tiffany said, pausing, then thinking back to the number of answers she'd heard Chris volunteer in middle school science. "You couldn't have been."

"You heard it. Jesus." Chris shook his hand out. "It felt like something bit me."

Was this part of his act? Did he palm a little firework when she wasn't looking and blow himself up to buy some sympathy? It seemed more likely than an electric shock from a plastic handle. It was a joystick that she herself had used for hours on end, no shock.

She wouldn't have believed him, except that she didn't think he was a good enough actor to pull off the terrified look he had in his eye. He looked surprised and hurt, sucking on the webbing between his thumb and forefinger.

"Are you okay?" she asked. Being nice to Chris Murphy felt how she imagined passing kidney stones must feel.

"Yeah, I'm fine, but someone should load this thing onto the back of a garbage truck. It's too old to be fun, plus it's dangerous."

Hearing him badmouth *Ms. Pac-Man* was the last straw. Injury or not, it was time for this conversation to end.

"Well, I'm going to go," she said. To her astonishment he didn't try to stop her, just kept sucking his hand and staring at the machine.

"Okay. I'll see you," he said, now acting oddly civil, post-jolt. "I'm going to go find that retard. Someone's got to fix this thing before it kills someone."

He turned and walked down the aisle, back toward the stairs to the bowling alley.

Tiffany didn't leave the arcade, it was too early for that, but she did resolve to spend the rest of her tokens playing Skee-Ball. Skee-Ball was downstairs next to the restaurant and ticket redemption area, a place where she would be surrounded by people.

People other than Chris Murphy.

CHAPTER 2

In the five years he'd been the maintenance man at Funcave, Boden had seen arcade cabinets broken by destructive teenagers, but he had never seen one break down on its own. It wasn't that the cabinets were built to last, they weren't, but the machines at Funcave had a way of keeping themselves in check. He'd replace the occasional light bulb, switch out one or two flippers on the pinball machines every few months, but other than that the place seemed to take care of itself.

"It's right over here," the ruddy teen said, pointing to the second aisle, leading the way as Boden limped along behind him. The kid mumbled a few words that sounded nasty and Boden thought about hitting him in the back of his spiky-hair with his wrench. He touched his right pinky finger to his tool belt, reassured by the cold metal.

"I know where it is," Boden said, slurring at the end of the statement. Certain sounds were hard to pronounce when the right half of your face was paralyzed.

He didn't need the kid to tell him where *Ms. Pac-Man* was. He'd been here on the day they'd brought her in. That was downstairs, actually, when the game had been a new release. He was unsure if this was even the same cabinet. It probably was, just with all new parts, accounting for however many replacements and refurbishments had happened in the intervening years.

Boden could have used some refurbishment himself, someone to clean the carbon off his fading CRT tube. Decades ago, when this machine was new, Boden's face didn't droop and his right arm and leg didn't go dead if he forgot to massage them for twenty minutes every morning.

Strokes weren't just something that happened to grandpas. They happened to middle-aged unmarried guys who played too many video games, too. Boden had learned that the hard way, slumping over a game of *Joust* and waking up with the side of his head shaved and a shunt imbedded in his brain.

The shunt sounded cool on paper; it was inorganic matter coupled to his flesh and blood to keep him alive. Like what Tony Stark had. Sadly it didn't improve his reflexes or make the Bionic Man noise when he bent down to take a shit. What it did do was give him a blazing headache if he tried to focus on one thing for too long. Focus on something like, say, a video game.

No. Dan Boden, one-time northeast regional *Mappy* champion and editor emeritus of one of the web's oldest and finest classic video game scoreboards, could no longer play video games. He'd taken the maintenance position, offered by Eddie Harmon out of pity, not because of the spectacular pay, but because he wanted to be around the games he loved. There were days where he felt a little bit like a eunuch working at a brothel.

"It was a fucking thunderclap, man. Then *zap!*" the kid said, gesticulating with the middle fingers of both hands. Boden couldn't tell if the kid was conscious of the double-bird or not. It could well be his fingers' operative mode.

Boden leaned his good elbow against the cabinet, thankful for the moment's rest before he had to slouch down and poke around inside of *Ms. Pac-Man*.

"What are you waiting for?" the boy said from behind him.

"For you to go away so I can do my job," Boden said. This was the kind of kid that never learned or cared for that "respect your elders" thing. In fact, he looked like the kind of dull-eyed bully that might more readily ascribe to the "stomp your elders, especially if they're infirmed" philosophy.

"You should just be lucky I'm not suing. I'd own this place and all these shitty games. Demolish it and turn it into a titty bar."

Boden flinched. Now he really wanted to use that wrench.

"Stay if you want, then. There won't be much to see."

The machine had had its front-plate removed so often that there was a gap between the corners where the front clung loosely. It would take two hands to move, one to hold the plate up so it wouldn't slip off and spill tokens everywhere, the other to operate the key. Dan had not had full mobility in it for years, had time to get used to it, but still felt embarrassed when he had to use his right hand.

Using his left, he pressed the right flat against the machine. He uncurled the fingers of his right hand one by one and laid them flush with the particleboard. It was as if his hand belonged to someone else, like he was trying to set up a mannequin display. When that was done, he wrestled the key ring from his belt, his arm shaking under the weight of his torso.

"Do you, like, need a hand?" the kid said, possibly oblivious to the pun.

"No," Boden said, sounding meaner than he meant to. "This is my job, I do it every day by myself."

After what felt like a week, he found the correct key on the ring and plugged its round end into the hole on the coin door. The joint of his right wrist felt like it was lined with broken glass. He wanted to get off his knees, take a seat and massage his joints back to life for the next hour, but that wasn't an option with the kid mouth-breathing over his shoulder.

The only small blessing was that most of the machines at the Funcave had been modified so that they could be worked on by removing the coin door and without having to turn the machine around and access the back.

"You wanted to help? Now you can help. Pick this up and lay it—gently—over there." Boden pointed to the machine across from them, a stand-up *Joust II* cabinet. It wasn't the machine that he'd stroked-out playing, that had been a sit-down "cocktail cabinet" model of the original *Joust*, but the association was strong enough to make him cringe.

The kid did as he was told, lifting up the modified front panel and moving it to the opposite side of the aisle. Boden kept a hand cupped under the coin return so nothing spilled out.

Boden's first impression of the inside of *Ms. Pac-Man* was that the machine was so clean it glistened. In the low light of the classic arcade, it would have been possible to suspend your disbelief, believe that it was 1987, Devo on the radio, and the weight of the quarters in your pocket tugging at the waistband of your jeans. For that brief moment, Boden felt no pain in his wrist and knee.

"Agh, it stinks!" The kid's voice ripped Dan out of his stupor. "It's like something died in there."

Boden could barely smell it. He only had a shade of his former olfactory senses remaining, and that was impeded by the wealth of nose hair that he would one day have to get around to trimming.

He took the miniature flashlight from his keychain and clicked it on. The beam cut through the gloom of the arcade and showed the guts of the machine as they were, not as he wished them to be.

His first appraisal was correct: the circuits and wires that ran *Ms. Pac-Man* did glisten. They were covered with a fine layer of slime. Boden dipped his head under the lip that housed the joystick and bent so that his head and right arm were inside the cabinet.

Hairy nostrils or not, he could smell it now. It wasn't as the kid had described it, though. The air of the cabinet didn't carry the necrotic stink of putrefaction, but instead the breath of new life. It did happen to be the fungal, spore-releasing breath of new life, but mushrooms counted as life.

"Yep," Boden said, resisting the temptation to add "there's yer problem" like he was some yokel mechanic.

"Fucking disgusting. This place should be condemned."

"Calm yourself," Boden said. The kid was an odd duck. For someone who talked like he was disinterested in the workings of the machine, he'd insisted on watching it opened up. Also, as someone who had twice in the last twenty minutes called for the closing of the arcade, Boden recognized his pimply face, was used to seeing the boy hang around for hours on end.

"I've seen this in one or two of the other machines, but never this bad," Boden said, lying. It was only a small lie, though. He'd actually seen some level of this buildup in *all* the machines, but if he told the kid that the health department might be showing up and closing the place down. The fungus didn't seem to hurt the way the machines functioned, so if it was safe for them it was probably safe for humans.

"What is it?" the kid asked, he was down on his knees now too, had shifted the chains on his black cargo shorts so he could kneel comfortably. It had been a while since Boden had seen a kid dress like that. He was a weird kind of half-goth who probably considered himself too butch to wear the makeup, but was still into the black and chains.

Boden reached his hand up to grab a bit of the fleshy lichen that was growing on the sides of the circuit board. It felt spongy and unreal, similar to the foam latex people used to make Halloween masks.

"You're touching it?" the kid said. "Without gloves? Come on, you're going to get sick or something." For a guy who had a Jason Voorhees hockey mask poorly tattooed on his forearm, this kid was kind of a pussy.

The goo was warm, and as it slid down Boden's fingers he swore that it tingled, giving him a low-grade electric charge. The hair on his knuckles began to rise and that was enough to get him to wipe it on his khakis. The stuff left a translucent, slightly chromatic stain, like a giant slug had crawled across his leg, a trail of rainbow sputum behind it.

"I'll get a few rags from the supply closet and come wipe this down."

"What about my hand? The shock?"

"What's wrong with it?" Boden asked.

"Nothing, I guess." The kid stared at his open fist, closed it again, the skin wasn't even red anymore.

"It was an isolated incident." Boden said, using his sleeve to daub the side of his mouth, there was a dot of drool there that he didn't want spilling down his chin. "These things get moldy sometimes, especially when we've had a lot of humidity. I'll go through and clean them out over the next week."

"This jizz is the reason I got hurt?"

Boden sighed. This was the longest conversation he'd had with anyone in the last three months. That should have been a wakeup call that he needed to get out more often.

"I've never seen the crud get this bad. You were probably sweating onto the joystick, it dribbled down and hit this stuff, created a closed circuit with the A/C supply and gave you a pop. No biggie, it didn't even turn off the game, right?"

"Yeah, right." The kid looked sullen, maybe because he'd just realized that their time together was coming to a close. "I'm Chris, by the way."

"Dan." He put out his hand.

"You should wash your hands, Dan." Chris said, then balled his fists, put them in the pockets of his sweatshirt and walked away.

He could have at least stuck around to help Boden close up the machine.

CHAPTER 3

Chris had never taken the time to talk to the handyman. He had seen him limping around the arcade and figured that he was mute or retarded or something. It was probably the way that Dan stared glassy-eyed at the machines whenever kids were playing them that had caused Chris to write the guy off as a simp, possibly a pervert.

He wasn't that bad, as cripples went.

Helping with the machine had felt like an adventure, even if it was a minor one, and it had broken the monotony of Chris's usual Funcave routine. By this time in the afternoon, he'd have usually played a round of *Time Crisis* (a game that was old, but still cool because you got to use a light gun that looked close enough to the real thing) and eaten a pizza. His stomach grumbled at the thought of microwave-rubberized cheese.

To get to the food counter he had to pass the Skee-Ball. He gave Tiffany a quick nod, but couldn't tell if she noticed him or not. She wasn't white, but damn was she cute.

A man could not live on white bread alone, Chris's dad once told him while licking his lips. His father was also quick to add that Chris would find himself disowned if he ever thought of marrying a black or a Jew. Or if he turned queer.

Chris's father was a shithead.

Chris Murphy was more of a mama's boy, even though she was dead now. The Jason tattoo on his arm was put there to honor her memory. He thought she'd appreciate it more than a heart that said mother. It had cost him two week's pay.

Sometimes he daydreamed about hacking people up, like Jason Voorhees did, then hallucinating his mother and her giving him a big, imaginary hug. He'd mow down all the dickheads that gave him wide berth in the lunchroom, the ones that neglected to come to his birthday party from age six through twelve. She was the one throwing them, so after his mom croaked he'd stopped having birthday parties.

The girl behind the pizza counter was concentrating on looking disinterested. She probably thought it made her appear mysterious and unattainably beautiful, but Chris thought that all it did was make her look like a stuck-up bitch.

"Can I help you?" she asked.

He'd ordered a personal pan pepperoni pizza from this counter at least three days a week for the last three-plus years, ever since he'd qualified for his learner's permit. The girl had still not picked up on this or, if she had, was not the type to say: "Hey Chris, will it be the usual today?"

Just once he'd like to hear her say that. Even an infrequent smile might save her from his inevitable Camp Crystal Lake massacre.

"One personal pizza with pepperoni." He didn't add a please, certainly wasn't going to drop any of his change in the tip jar. It would only go to cocaine and lip gloss and he wasn't comfortable supporting that kind of behavior.

He imagined her snorting a line off of Tiffany Park's ass, him standing by and watching until they were finished and then making them kiss. His mind was like this at times, prone to fits of acute perversion. He sometimes wondered if other guys thought the same way, then he took a glance at the subreddits he subscribed to, how many followers they had, and guessed that most men did.

The girl groaned at being made to leave her seat behind the counter, walked two steps and got him an already-boxed pizza out of the rotating heater. The restaurant seemed to have a full kitchen back there, but Chris had never seen anything more complicated than French fries and mozzarella sticks come out of it. Even in those situations the counter clerks worked the fryer. There was no chef at the Funcave.

The tiny pizza's were microwaved and then kept hot in the spinner. It looked like they had room for an oven back there. Cheap bastards. The pizza's weren't that bad, as long as you told yourself you weren't eating pizza, you were eating a pizza-inspired snack.

"Anything to drink?"

"A Pepsi." It was always a Pepsi. She should know that.

She filled the cup with too much ice and couldn't be bothered to press the plastic lid down correctly.

"Five fifty-nine," she said and Chris handed her a five and a single.

He took a seat facing the wall but kept an eye on the mirror that pointed out to the arcade floor. Tiffany was still at Skee-Ball, seemingly oblivious to the entire world save for those eight wooden balls and that five-hundred point hole. She had a mound of tickets at her feet. The game didn't payout much, so he estimated that she'd been there the whole time he'd been upstairs talking to the gimp.

Behind her was the rest of the first floor arcade, some of the new machines spit out gobs of tickets. They were fancy casino games dressed up like old school-carnie games which provided just enough thrill to hook children into gambling. Beyond those were the newer arcade games, stuff that was not yet ancient enough to be part of the museum upstairs.

As he ate, a group of three teens arrived and crowded around the fighting games. The relative peace of the arcade was shattered by their cursing and screaming as they took turns on *Street Fighter Alpha* and *Mortal Kombat 3*. Two of the kids were black and none of them seemed particularly threatening, but there was still enough of his father's blood in him that Chris had never dared try to play with them. It was a shame because he was pretty good with Blanka, knew all of his special moves.

When he got bored with watching the black kids in the reflection, he boxed up his crusts, wiped his hands and stood up from the table. As he turned he watched Tiffany's head flick back to the Skee-Ball lane. She'd been watching him.

Ha! Caught you looking, my little China-girl. Chris Murphy smiled, a real smile, for the first time in days.

CHAPTER 4

Chris Murphy's smile was ringed with pizza grease, the sheen made his acne seem worse. Under the bright lights of the first floor, surrounded by other people, he didn't seem nearly as threatening. She could see now that his hair was not only spiked, the style that he'd kept since the early two thousands, but that his blonde roots were starting to grow in under his black dyejob. She imagined him applying hair dye in an effort to look more metal and the fear of him being a possible psycho killer stalker began to seem funny.

She could see out of the corner of her eye that he was standing still, smiling at her. She threw a ball down the lane and took a breath before he started moving again.

"That's a force! I had you, man!" one of the guys playing *Street Fighter* shouted from her left. It sounded like Jason Day from her Civics class. He shouted "That's a force, Miss!" every time their teacher assigned homework. It was kind of cute, kind of exhausting.

She looked at the glass double doors that led out to the parking lot and saw that the sky was darkening. She clicked on her phone to check the time. It was only five thirty, there must be a storm on its way, otherwise it wouldn't be that dark.

Tossing her last ball up the lane, it hit the ramp at just the right angle and sunk into the five-hundred point basket, nothing but net. A perfect game and she only got twenty tickets. These machines needed to be updated to properly compensate her for her mastery of the sport.

Gripping the end of the ticket, she gave a firm tug, able to wrest a bonus ticket from the mouth of the machine. She threw the stack of yellow tickets into her purse and shouldered the bag. She'd redeem them later, maybe never if Funcave didn't start stocking anything good to buy with them. Tiffany had enough Frisbees, shot glasses, and plastic spider-rings to last her ten lifetimes.

One of the glass doors squealed on its frame and Tiffany watched as Chris Murphy shouldered his way out of the arcade. Conflicting feelings of relief and disappointment washed over her. The attention had been nice, even if it seemed like the kind that would result in the boy traipsing around in front of a mirror singing show tunes and wearing her skin like a fur coat.

Bucking up, she realized that the upstairs arcade was now Murphy-free. It was too late in the day to weigh her purse down with another roll of tokens, so she scraped the bottom of her bag and came up with a measly two coins.

Better make them count, she told herself. *Maybe today is the day we see that kill screen.*

One of the boys waiting to get on *Street Fighter* whistled at her as she walked by, a white kid in a wife-beater and baggy pants.

"Damn girl, you need to get out of that sweatshirt and into something that shows off what I know you've got." He wiped his upper lip with one finger. What this gesture was meant to suggest, she had no idea. He was in his mid-twenties, but his mustache was so thin and unimpressive it looked like he'd drawn it on with a dull pencil. She didn't recognize him so he'd probably graduated or dropped out while she was still in middle school.

"Shut the fuck up," Jason said, still hunched over the machine with his back to her. "Super Combo!" the announcer shouted and Jason took the opportunity to slap the kid who'd whistled on his bare shoulder, the tips of his fingers leaving an angry red mark on the older kid's pale skin.

"He's sorry, Tiffany," Jason said, turning to face her but only for a second. When he turned back to the screen it sounded like he hadn't missed a beat.

Cute, brutishly chivalrous, and good at video games. Jason was a catch. She blushed and continued toward the stairs.

Upstairs, they'd turned the music up. Downstairs the radio was tuned to top-ten hits, a nosebleed-inducing tidal wave of shit: Chris Brown and Robin Thicke spitting lyrics that either directly or indirectly endorsed date rape. Upstairs it wasn't the radio, but instead the overhead speakers were hooked up to a massive CD-changer that played nothing but the classics: Flock of Seagulls, Squeeze, Blondie. Pure gaming tunes.

The divide was generational and economically-minded. The owner of Funcave wanted to keep both types of customer happy. Happy enough to keep dropping coins into machines. At eighteen, Tiffany was meant to enjoy the music downstairs, playing the newer games and socializing with her peers over a few frames of bowling and a pizza.

But her heart and soul belonged upstairs. Tiffany had not been alive for the golden era of video arcades, but she still felt strong nostalgia for days she'd never seen. Or maybe she liked this floor so much better because of the music. Because Lionel Ritchie was Mozart when compared to T-Pain.

Dan limped by her as she ducked down the aisle toward *Ms. Pac-Man*. He carried a bucket full of dirty dishrags and as he passed she could smell that he'd just cleaned up something gross. She said "hello" and he just smiled back. The lack of a hello didn't seem rude. He wore a look that said: "I'd say hi, but I need to lie down."

They weren't best buddies, but she'd see him watching her play sometimes and knew his name because it was sewn onto his shirt. He wasn't a creep staring at a teenage girl, he was more interested in what and how she was playing than anything else. She got the feeling that he knew the games well, that he'd offer her pointers if she'd ask.

The second floor was not as dead as it was when she'd been playing earlier. There was an assemblage of "regulars" tossing tokens into their favorite machines. Some of these men, and they were all men, held high scores in these games, some of those scores were world records. Most weren't playing for the records, though, most were playing because it was what they did.

They'd been gamers before their bellies had distended and their glasses had tripled in thickness. They'd been gamers when they were gangly teens in Rush t-shirts, before those same t-shirts were stained, moth-eaten, and worn with suspenders stretched over them.

The Regulars were admirable and pathetic, all at once.

It was all a matter of perspective as to whether or not they were creatures of habit or social cripples who would not, could not, let go of the past. Tiffany saw herself in forty years, her purse traded in for a fannypack, a green plastic visor shielding her eyes, her jowls set in a line of concentration as she chipped away at a run of *Ms. Pac-Man*. The image didn't disgust her. There was something noble in it.

Her two tokens went faster than she'd wanted them to. Both games had been unspectacular, she'd done okay, but she felt as if the guardian angel that sometimes watched over the machine, scooching the ghosts away at just the right moments, had taken the night off.

CHAPTER 5

The conscious electric current formerly known as Robby Asaro watched over the arcade, ever-present.

It had taken Robby forever to get such a strong foothold in the *Ms. Pac-Man* machine. That kid Chris was no good, Robby could feel the anger rolling off him, practically see it fizzling off in lines of heat. If the anger weren't enough, his antics had caused Dan to clean out the cabinet.

It didn't hurt, Dan Boden scrubbing the ectoplasm from the walls of the machine, just a minor tickling sensation, but the loss of his favorite machine was frustrating beyond description.

Because he could no longer watch Tiffany from inside the screen, he settled for peeking out at her from the machine behind. Even watching the back of her head was comforting, though he could not influence the game the way he was used to. He would need to reroute his work in the rest of the arcade, focus his energies on building back up inside the *Ms. Pac-Man* cabinet.

These Namco machines were easy to grow into anyway. They got a lot of play, a lot of love and respect and nostalgia shot at them from a lot of hearts and minds. It was easier to enter a game that was beloved.

Ghosts and Goblins had been a pain in the ass to get a hold of, everyone was always furious while playing it.

Being dead had been the best thing to ever happen to Robby Asaro. Not dying, that part had been terrible, was still terrible because he relived it every night after the lights were shut off and the games were unplugged and he had nothing with which to occupy himself.

For the first few months he was dead, Robby had spent all of his time in the pizza oven. That wasn't fun—at all—and the day that Mr. Harmon had the oven dismantled and taken away had been a momentous occasion. Robby was no longer tethered to the machine, could feel himself floating around the first floor of the arcade like an astronaut in zero gravity. Every time he'd float near a machine he could feel a kind of magnetic pull, would have to push off with all his might to free himself and keep on floating.

He didn't have arms and legs anymore, was more of a whirling ball of thought and feeling than anything else, so once he'd realized that he was being drawn to anything electronic, that he could use the machines to weigh pieces of himself down, he became the spider of Funcave. Or maybe more like Spider-Man.

The more people that visited his machines, the better he felt. The more machines he left a little part of himself in, the bigger his network—his web—grew.

He was everywhere at once, his attention torn between the boys playing *Street Fighter* downstairs; Hank, the fifty-two year old man playing *Missile Command*; his buddy Yosef plowing his way through a later level of *Gauntlet*; and Tiffany Park, the princess of the arcade. That was not her official title and he doubted anyone felt that way but him. But a princess she was.

By the power vested in him, as the God of the arcade, Robby decreed it.

He needed some mood music, so he jumped into the back office of Funcave where the CD player was housed. Because Robby was everywhere and nowhere, jumping around the building was only quasi-traveling. It was more shifting his perception to another area that he controlled. Like opening an eye that you'd been keeping closed, only Robby had thousands of eyes.

In the office, Eddie Harmon was bent over his desk, frantically masturbating to images on his laptop. Robby could control the laptop if he wanted to and occasionally used it look up information he needed about different games, but mostly he kept out of there.

Eddie's porno collection made it a seedy place to spend any extended period of time.

Robby dove into the CD changer and swung the carousel around until it stopped at the disc he wanted. With a small *zap* that took no effort at all, he interrupted the song that'd been playing and switched it with Depeche Mode's "Just Can't Get Enough". At the game, Tiffany's back straightened. He couldn't see her face but would bet that she was smiling.

Robby had watched her grow throughout the years and her tenure at Funcave was nearly as old as his. That was, as an electric current, not back when he'd been paid to be there, when he'd been alive.

She was a pretty young girl, but the attraction wasn't sexual, quite the contrary, Tiffany was the child he'd never had.

Her tenth birthday party downstairs in the bowling alley, but she had cried because all she really wanted to do was play the big-kid games upstairs. When all the other kids had grown up, grown tired of hanging around the arcade and traded video games for beer and parties, Tiffany had stayed true.

Tiffany was a skilled gamer. Robby knew it, had seen her play. He bent the rules for her sometimes, but it was only to encourage her, foster the greatness that he knew she was capable of achieving.

He loved the regular customers too, but they had been great before Robby had gotten to know them. Tiffany was the only one he'd gotten to see mature and he looked forward to her induction into the trophy case.

Without the infrastructure to make changes to the machine, ride the circuit board to victory alongside her, Tiffany's games were disappointingly brief.

It was his own damn fault, too. If Robby hadn't shocked that boy, she would have been playing *Ms. Pac-Man* right now. Tiffany was tough, would have gotten the boy to leave her alone without his help. She was clearly not interested. Then she would have gone back to playing, with Robby watching over her character. Inside the machine he'd tick a few ones to zeros and vice versa, bending the game to his will as she enjoyed extra lives and some late-game play.

It was too late for that now, he'd made his decision and now she was leaving the arcade. Robby jumped through each machine on the way to the parking lot, staring out of the screens and watching her go out into the rainy night, all alone.

Drive safely, Robby thought, and kept watching her from inside the coin-pusher machine that pointed toward the first-floor doorway.

One day he thought he might try hopping into her car battery, have her take him home to meet her real parents. But that day was a ways off, he told himself.

He still had plenty of work to get done in the arcade.

CHAPTER 6

It had seemed like such a good idea at the time, waiting for Tiffany to come out of the arcade and offering to walk her to her car, but then it had begun to rain.

Chris could feel the styling gel leaving his hair and running down his forehead as it mixed with the raindrops. He'd tried to wipe it off at first, but that had only made his hands sticky. He thought about going back inside the arcade where it was dry, but then he'd look even weirder milling around the door, lurking.

He decided to give her fifteen more minutes, if she wasn't out by then he'd climb into his truck and head home.

As if she'd done it on purpose, in order to make him stand in the rain for the maximum amount of time he'd agreed to, Tiffany walked out of the arcade exactly fifteen minutes later.

Pushing off from where he'd pressed himself flat against the façade of the building he saw that his body had left a dry outline on the brick. His clothes were heavy with rainwater, his hair flat against his forehead, moistened into bangs. At least he wouldn't need to shower when he got home.

He waited until he was a few soggy footsteps from her back before saying anything.

"Hey there," he said.

She jumped straight up, then whirled around. He must have scared her. She made a face upon seeing him

"Here," he said, offering her a wad of junk mail circulars and coupons that he'd scraped off the floor of his truck. He'd kept them under his shirt to keep them dry. She looked at the papers like she wasn't sure what he wanted her to do with them so he held them over his own head to show her.

"Oh, I'm okay, thanks," she said and leaned out toward the rest of the parking lot like she wanted to keep walking.

"Mind if I walk with you?" he asked. She made a face that told him she was unsure how to respond. Damn it, he was blowing the whole thing! "My car's out that way too," he added.

"Okay," she said. She already had her keys in her hand and gripped them tighter, wrapping the key ring around one of her fingers and making the knuckle glow white.

"Do you ever go anywhere but this place?" he asked as they walked, Tiffany avoiding puddles, him splashing right through them. His boots were soaked anyway, why try to step around them?

"Huh?" She was acting purposefully aloof. He didn't like it. Waiting for her had been sweet. He'd never tried something like that before. Why wouldn't she give him a fucking break?

"I mean, like, do you ever go out to eat or go to the movies or anything?"

"Not often," she said, thumbing a button on her keychain and causing a car to beep in the distance. It was dark, but there weren't many cars in the lot and what few there were huddled under one of the two dim lampposts. Still he couldn't tell which one was hers, but they were getting closer to it by the sound of the beep. Automatic locks, fancy.

Her body language told him that she was getting ready to hop in and drive away as soon as they got there. The time-crunch was scrambling his brain, making him forget all the lines that he'd prepared, making him lose his cool.

"I have a truck and a boombox, we should go to the drive-in sometime," he said. "It's fun."

The locks on his truck were manual, had to be opened up by using a good old-fashioned key, not a remote control like her expensive Jap car. He'd paid for his truck too, not much, but he was betting that Tiffany Park's car had come from her parents. Maybe it had arrived as a gift with a big bow on it. Like in the commercials.

"Yeah. Maybe we could. When the weather's better," she said, nearly as soaked as he was now. She readjusted her grip on her purse, bringing the rain slick straps further up her shoulder. Was she still upset about when he'd been keeping it from her? He'd only held on to the bag to get her to stay around longer, so he could spend time with her. Why didn't she see that?

"Cool," he said, but he didn't believe her, she was just trying to get rid of him.

"I'm right there," she said, pointing to the car next to her. "So I'll see you later, Chris. Okay?" Her words were sugary now, but there was a condescending tone that he didn't like.

He reached out and grabbed her shoulder. Outside of when he brushed her hand when they were playing the game earlier, it was the first time he'd ever made a conscious decision to touch a girl.

"You're already wet, why don't you just give me a second to say what I'm trying to say?" he asked.

"Please take your hand off me." Her voice was cold again and he could see that the way she was holding her keys had changed once more. She had three keys clenched in her fist, in between her three middle fingers, forming a dinky version of Wolverine's claws.

"Whoa, cool it. I'm asking you if you'd like to go on a date. It's not like I'm attacking you or anything."

"That's fine, but please take your hand off me."

This was all going so wrong. There was no way he was cutting and running, taking his hand away now.

"Don't tell me what to fucking do. I'm not looking to rape you or something, put your keys down and talk to me for a second."

She reeled her hand back and punched him, not hard, but quick enough that it caught him off guard. The keys scraped along the thin skin under his left eye, tearing it up. The pain was immediate and vast.

"Are you fucking kidding me?" he screamed. It was too early to tell if she'd blinded him. He didn't wait to find out, didn't wait to think. The back of his knuckles brushed against her jaw, the tips of his fingers banging against her lips and teeth as he followed through.

Fuck, what did I do? It was the last thought he had before she started screaming for help. Her voice made him feel small, terrible, and insane with anger. If she would have just given him a minute to talk to her.

He looked at her, unable to tell how much damage he'd done by the flickering glow of the light overhead. It was possible that some of the blood on her face was his.

The streetlamp hadn't been flashing before they'd started fighting. He looked up to investigate what was going on, his adrenaline-soaked mind telling him that it might be a police helicopter.

The light shone unnaturally bright and he wondered if she hadn't given him a concussion that'd caused him to start hallucinating. The light began to strobe above him and he didn't wonder anything else.

Since the bolt traveled at the speed of light—faster than sound—Chris Murphy didn't hear what killed him.

§

The light was the brightest thing Tiffany had ever seen, the flash burning the look of horror from Chris's face into her retinas in a blue and white negative.

The arch of blue lightning came out of nowhere, louder than a gunshot. Crossing the parking lot, Tiffany had not heard any thunder, but then again her mind had not been on her surroundings, but on the boy following her to her car during a rainstorm.

Tiffany could feel her scalp hum as the electricity in the air struck down through Chris's skull, down to his boots and then shot out of his face, the overhanging lamppost working like a lightning rod to wick the bolt back into the air.

Chris was able to keep on his feet for a moment after the current left his body, his knees locking up and keeping him upright. Only for a moment, though, then the weight of his smoking head dragged him back down to earth, his body crumpling backwards into a foul-smelling heap.

He was flesh and blood, but he didn't smell like cooked meat as much as he did burning plastic and fresh-poured asphalt.

She looked at the soles of his feet, the bottoms of his boots were melted strings, some strands still connected to the tarmac. The tips of his fingers were black and singed, two of them had popped, the ends looking like an exploding cigar in a cartoon.

Screaming was her first reaction, getting him help her second. Her third was realizing, looking at the chard holes of his eyes, that help could only come in the form of a priest, if he'd been religious at all.

Chris Murphy was as dead as one could possibly be. Killed by a bolt of lightning that hadn't even been strong enough to blow out the bulb in the lamppost.

After a second to let her body stop feeling numb, she put one foot in front of the other and walked back toward the arcade.

She didn't realize she was crying until Jason Day was asking her what had happened.

"We heard you scream," he said. Her shoulders were dryer now, and the rain had stopped pelting the top of her head. She was inside, with Jason's zip-up sweatshirt wrapped around her, her sopping wet one staining the carpet at her feet. She didn't think she'd lost consciousness because she was still standing, but each passing moment became like a half-remembered dream, shifting in and out of her mind as if it may or may not have happened.

Dan was there, too. His face looked even worse when he was frowning, the edge of his mouth drooping unnaturally low. He was wet, must have come in from the rain. "Someone needs to call an ambulance," he said, his slur heavy enough that it was hard to understand him. He didn't say why it couldn't be him that called, everyone knew.

Jason looked behind Tiffany, handing his cell phone to the boy who'd whistled at her less than an hour ago. "Do it, Cal. Dial nine-one-one and tell them there's been some kind of accident."

The image of Chris dying under the lamp was burned into her eyes, dimming the world around her with its comparative brightness. Dimming an already gloomy world because the overhead lights in the arcade were off. The only light was the glow of the machines, which was odd because you'd figure that the light bulbs would be more important to keep running than the games.

"What the fuck is going on down here?" a voice asked from beyond the small crowd that had gathered around Tiffany. She'd only ever seen the owner of Funcave a few times, he seemed to spend most of his time behind a closed door that said "Employees Only", but Tiffany recognized him as he nudged Dan out of the way to get a look at her.

"A kid's in the parking lot, Eddie," Dan said.

"There always seem to be kids in the parking lot, Boden." The fat man said. He wore a stained polo shirt, but instead of the Lacoste alligator or Polo pony stitched over his heart, the Atari symbol stood out white on black.

Dan (or Boden, either his nickname or a last name) tried to lean in to whisper so Tiffany couldn't hear.

She spoke up and saved him the trouble of having to whisper without getting spittle all over his boss's ear: "He's dead. Struck by lightning, I think."

Jason and his other friend made a gasping noise, nobody must have known but Dan and Tiffany.

Cal had walked to the door to use the phone, but was yelling into it anyway. "Hello. I'm at the Funcave on Route 1. Someone's been struck by lightning I think, please send an ambulance." The boy looked and sounded like a hillbilly, even if his diction was straight-laced, polite and tinged with booklearnin'.

Eddie, the owner, spoke next. "There's a kid out there who's been struck by lightning and you're all in here taking care of the girl who didn't? He may not be dead, you don't know."

Dan looked about to say something but Eddie used a hairy arm to knock him out of the way, nearly toppling him. "Someone help me move him inside, he's gonna fucking drown out there in this rain."

Tiffany wanted to say more, wanted to describe how deep she'd seen into Chris's head through his eye sockets, but the thought of it put her out, dragged her under.

Jason got a hand on her before she hit her head, but she blinked out of consciousness before they could place her down to the carpet.

CHAPTER 7

God! It hurt so much. Everything Chris Murphy had been, still was, poured into Robby.

The boy was dead before he hit the pavement, but part of him had held on to the lightning and traveled back into the lamppost.

A black wave of sadness and hate hit Robby as he ran from the scene of the crime. He jumped from car to car, causing engines to roar to life and security alarms to sound, headed back to the safety of his arcade. He couldn't escape the hate, though, it was part of him now.

The shock from the *Ms. Pac-Man* machine had only been a precursor to this. Murder. Robby had ended a life. In defense of someone who was innocent, someone he loved, that was true, but he'd still made a conscious decision to kill.

Words he'd never used before, never even thought, bubbled into his mind, a whole new lexicon. Cunt! *How could you do this you simp dick sucker? Protecting that little chink cocktease. Pathetic.* They were his thoughts, he'd admit it, but the words, the sentiment contained within would never have belonged to him. Robby was still one entity, but he felt new and *not* improved. His thoughts were base and disgusting. He needed to vomit but had no mouth. No stomach for that matter.

He felt drained and confused, but he needed to keep the power going to his games, they gave him the strength to think better. After the momentary power outage, he jumped from the last car in the lot back to inside the walls of the arcade, bringing the games back with him.

Inside *Street Fighter Alpha*, he watched as Cal berated his friend Jason. "Now it comes back on, of course it cuts out the one time I was going to get you. Shit."

Jason shushed him. "Do you hear that?"

Cal and Robby both listened, Robby straining to hear the outside world beyond the screen. Concentrating on something helped him forget the pain, the nausea of having Chris's hate settling inside of him.

Chris's feelings and memories were trying to take root, dirt settling to the bottom of a glass of water. Robby was troubled by the pictures, old and new, swirling around his building-sized consciousness.

He could form the images of people he'd never met, places he'd never been. Chris Murphy's father wiped Steel Reserve from his upper lip and called his son a faggot for spending more time with his Xbox than he did with his truck. Chris wedging an M-80 between the shell of his sister's pet turtle. Chris crying about it afterwards, burying the pieces. Chris's mother helping him blow out candles at a sparsely attended birthday party, one that had been held here in this building.

Robby feared that the feeling would last indefinitely. He needed to know whether all of the memories from the boy's sad, short, brutish life would rerun forever through his mind. The guilt and horror would drive him insane within a day.

Focusing on the sounds from the parking lot helped, if only because he could puzzle out what they were without hearing much of them. Outside, Tiffany was screaming for help.

Jason was the first to leave the machine, his friends David and Cal a few steps after him. Before he left, Cal pinched a quarter underneath the base of his joystick, holding his spot at the machine, still oblivious to how serious the situation was about to get.

From a different angle, Robby could see Dan Boden, also on his way to respond to the screams, albeit much slower than the boys. *Super-gimp to the rescue!* Aside from Tiffany, Dan was Robby's favorite person at Funcave. He was a man who'd been knocked around by life, had what he'd loved most taken away from him, but still tried to keep it in his world. Dan was a man to be respected, not mocked.

It was impossible to see into the darkness of the parking lot, not without jumping outside the walls of the arcade, but the first group to arrive back was Jason, Cal and David. Jason and Cal flanked Tiffany, the two taller boys holding her up so only the tips of her toes were moving across the ground. She moved her legs, so out of it that she seemed to think she was walking, not being carried by the two boys.

They came to a halt and set her down, on her feet, her knees and spine drooping low under the restored weight of her body. She waved them off when they told her to sit down.

Tiffany's complexion had always been pale, but her paleness was now discolored. She'd gone beyond white and was now alternating colors of green and blue. Her lips were dark, shivering like she'd just been pulled out of an icy lake. Jason peeled off his sweatshirt and swapped it for her own.

The sight of Jason's dark hand touching Tiffany's pale skin stirred a hatred in Robby that was not his own, a hate that had been passed down for generations in the Murphy family and one that Chris was alternatively attracted to and ashamed of.

Dan came back a few minutes later, his right side looking even more deflated than when he'd left.

Jason waved his phone at Cal and asked him to call an ambulance. *Too late for that*, Robby thought with something sickeningly akin to pride.

After that, Eddie Harmon appeared, his voice full of bluster. Robby guessed that he was looking for Dan in order to yell at him about the lights. He'd probably lost his internet connection, too. Fat piece of shit pervert.

Only some of those were Robby's feelings, but he'd never voice them that way. Eddie had not been responsible for his accident, the one that had sent him through the fire all those years ago, but right now it felt like it. He wanted to hate someone, and Eddie's loud mouth, constant jerking off, and pus-gut made it easy for it to be him.

Robby imagined what Eddie would look like after as much voltage as he'd sent into Chris Murphy, whether he'd pop like a carnival game balloon as the current flowed through him, searching for a way out.

Before Robby had time to react, Eddie and David were out the door going to check on Chris. David threw the hood of his sweatshirt up over his shaved head to protect from the rain. Robby hated them both for what they intended to do, they wanted to sully his arcade by bringing Chris Murphy's toasted body inside.

Robby imagined flecks of Chris's blackened skin flaking off of his fingers and landing on the pristine carpet. He envisioned cinders floating into the air ducts, swirling into the lungs of the building and giving his arcade a cancer.

Robby could not allow that to happen.

CHAPTER 8

The metal security gate was farther up than it had to be to cover the doors. Eddie had problems with kids, probably kids that looked a lot like David, spray painting the sign above the door. The sign was custom machined, expensive, and a pain to get repainted, so the solid metal gate stretched four feet up above the top of the door, tall enough to cover the sign.

Right now this security gate was closing with them on the wrong side of it, stuck in the rain.

"You need to hurry up, man," David said. They'd only introduced themselves a second ago, while on their way to pick up the injured kid's body, but now the black youth felt comfortable enough with Eddie to call him "man". Eddie didn't like that.

The Murphy kid was dead, that was for sure, but Eddie had made such a big deal about bringing him inside they'd had to try.

Eddie felt sweat beading against his balding head, mingling with the steady fall of rain. Even burnt up, the kid was heavier than he looked. Eddie belonged to a gym, had for three years, but only went about once every six months, sometimes less.

"Why the fuck is the gate moving?" Eddie said, puffing with exertion.

"Does it matter? Come on," David said. The boy held the body by its armpits and tugged at his end to hurry Eddie along, almost ripping the legs out of his grip. Melted kid smudged the sides of Eddie's pants, soaking through the dead boy's socks.

Eddie looked up, the sign was completely covered by the gate now, in thirty seconds the motor would press the bottom flush against the ground.

The doors opened to the inside and Dan propped one open with his shoe and waved them in from the doorway.

"Why did you close it?" Eddie yelled, his hands caked with boiled gelatinous blood. He'd gripped the corpse below the knees, but the slime was pushing up through the fabric of the kid's black pants. It felt good to yell at Dan Boden, normalized the situation.

"We didn't touch it. The power's acting weird, hurry."

David ducked low so he didn't bump his head on the bottom of the falling gate. With the next step Eddie took the mechanical grinding of the gate's gears stopped, freezing the gate on a height with the man's forehead.

"That was close," Eddie said, taking another step forward, both Dan and the other black kid helping David take up the load. Their Joe-Bob-looking friend was still on the phone with the nine-one-one call center.

There was a sound like a metal cable snapping and the gate dropped its hundred pound load into freefall.

The gate broke both of the corpse's legs at the knee and smashed Eddie Harmon's hands so badly that the joints of his wrists popped like glass bottles in a vise. The elasticity of his skin and tendons was still strong enough to drag him flat to his belly, knock the wind out of his lungs, and trap him under the gate.

Shards of bone sticking through the skin, all because he was trying to do the right thing, Eddie Harmon cried out for help.

The ambulance was still seven minutes away.

CHAPTER 9

Neither Yosef nor Hank heard the commotion going on downstairs.

Hank *had* noticed the change in lighting upstairs in the classic game room, but was in too deep with his game of *Discs of Tron* to investigate.

The music had stopped for about fifteen seconds, but had resumed right where it'd left off: Dexy's Midnight Runners imploring Eileen to come on. Or telling his friends what to do to her. Either way.

Hank could spend days in the arcade, totally would if they kept it open twenty-four hours. There were days that he'd get to Funcave straight from work, then forget to eat until it was closing time at eleven. Those nights he'd stop at the McDonald's on the way home and binge with two Big Macs, a twenty piece McNuggets and a large Coke. He still weighed only one-fifty, though, so he figured that all the nervous energy he expelled playing games helped him keep off the pounds.

He worked at the Arby's near Milton, but at night, on his way home, the only fast food he wanted was Micky-D's.

The power outage ten minutes ago had been frustrating, but now he was on such an epic run that he didn't care. Between level transitions he craned his head to see if Boden was around, he'd want to see this. Hank hadn't missed a single point and, although it may have been premature, thought this might turn out to be a historic enough run to make it onto Boden's website.

The spinners on the machine had always played loose, not as responsive as they had been in 1983 when the game had been released. Today they seemed snugger, rejuvenated. Either Dan had ordered replacement parts or Hank was just in-tune with the spirit tonight.

He was sweating, his fingers slipping on the hard plastic Frisbees that controlled the machine, but not even that messed him up.

"Hey Yosef," he yelled.

"Yeah," Yosef replied. The chubby dude was still chipping away at *Centipede*. Hank had once tried to tell him that the record was unattainable, unbeatable scores had already been reached and Yosef wasn't going to be one of them, but he didn't want to hear it. Hank's friend lacked the discipline to do well, he was good but he wanted to dance his way through every game by the seat of his pants. You couldn't play a game like *Centipede* by feeling alone: it was all about studying the patterns, memorization and strategy. Yosef had a habit of splitting the Centipede too early, impatient with waiting for it to descend.

"Is it hot in here, or is it just me?" Hank used a finger to clear the fog off of his glasses.

"The lights are off, maybe the A/C is, too." Yosef said.

Hank looked up, for the first time noticing that they were standing in the dark. Down the aisles, screens and marquees were the only light. Hank had always imagined that this was what the arcade looked like when it was closed, the lights off but the machines kept on. He knew that this was wrong, though, the machines were unplugged every night not only to save energy but to preserve the integrity of the tubes.

He looked back at the screen just in time to see himself struck with a disc. *Shit, derezzed.*

"Well, there goes that," Hank said to himself. Once he'd lost momentum like that, there was no regaining it. It was his fatal flaw as a gamer, once he slipped he never regained enough composure to keep going.

"What?" Yosef asked, his voice twisting the knife of defeat.

"Nothing. Play your fucking game." Hank tightened his grip

on the discs. He never took losing well, but he'd been raised right and would never yell out profanity in an arcade, within earshot of families. That was a slip he hadn't made since he was a kid.

There's no one around to hear, anyway. Say what you really feel. The voice startled Hank, because it was not Yosef's. He jumped back, taking his hands off the machine. He'd heard it inside his head, but it was not his own voice.

There was a metal clang and then the sound of panicked voices echoing up the stairwell that led downstairs. The volume of the music seemed to swell in response, strains of "Heart of Glass" drowning out the screams.

He put his hands back on the disc, frightened now and looking to the game for comfort.

"What the hell is going on?" Yosef said, standing behind Hank now. He'd abandoned his own game, probably a lost cause anyway, as Hank had always suspected all of his runs at *Centipede* were.

"I…don't…" Hank had no idea, so his words were placeholders until Yosef spoke again. Hank stared into Yosef's hairy face. There was wiry black fur all the places on his face but where it was supposed to be. Yosef could only grow a patchy, stringy beard, but the hair joining his eyebrows was plentiful. He didn't shave high enough on his cheeks, so there was a spot of hair between his eyes and his sideburns. Hank himself would never be Johnny Depp, but his friend was punishingly ugly.

"We should go check it out, it sounds like someone's hurt." Yosef said, having to yell over the music now. The track had cut over to a new song, not allowing Blondie to finish and the guitar of "Personal Jesus" starting up. Yosef's lone eyebrow fixed itself high in an expression of concern as the sounds from downstairs were drowned out.

Hank looked back at the screen, watched himself lose another life, his last. Game over. There was a static spark as his fingertip grazed one of the screws connecting the control panel to the rest of the cabinet.

There was an audible zap, but, upon thinking about it, what Hank had heard was a single word. *Kill.*

"Are you all right?" Yosef asked. They'd been friends for over twenty years, but right now Hank couldn't think why. Yosef was a loser. He didn't even have a job. He cashed disability checks for his tokens and took care of his sick mother during the day.

Pathetic. That was a word that Hank never used, because if he thought about it for any length of time, the word hit too close to home.

Yosef was still staring at him with that dumb look on his fuzzy face when Hank tossed a fist, wide and untrained, at his ear. Hank had never thrown a punch before in his life, so perhaps it was beginner's luck. Either that or Yosef had a glass jaw, because the bigger man dropped, his elbow smashing into the floor and the thin carpet doing very little to break his fall.

"What are you doing?" Yosef asked, so shocked at the idea of his friend hitting him that he was still not roused to fight-or-flight mode. That was a big mistake on his part, Hank grabbed a fistful of his beard with one hand, a mound of scalp with the other.

Why am I doing this? He asked. It was a good question, but not one that made him stop.

The clasps of Yosef's suspenders snagged on the carpet as Hank dragged the man along the floor, down the aisle to the *Centipede* cabinet.

Yosef's t-shirt was pulled up around his neck, his back must have been an excruciating mound of rug-burn.

The prone man's eyes went wild. He lashed out with an arm. Yosef had at least thirty pounds on Hank, but the lighter man still had the advantage. The disability checks hadn't been fraud: Yosef suffered from acute asthma.

"No," Yosef screamed between wheezes. It sounded like it was becoming hard to get enough air, Yosef's face was purple.

Yosef's nose buckled and spurt as Hank kicked him in the face.

Hank's New Balance sneakers were comfortable because they offered support for his high arches, but right now he wished he had a pair of steel-toed boots on so he could more effectively cave Yosef's head in.

"Why?" his friend asked again, some of his teeth broken or

chipped from the sound of it.

It was time to end this, Hank knew. No reason for cruelty. He helped Yosef to his feet.

Yosef was shaky, his knees wobbled and he listed to one side. Hank offered him an arm and he took it.

Why, given what had transpired over the last two minutes, would he take his arm?

Hank drew him close and then hit him in the throat with the blade of his hand. Yosef made a choking sound, his eyes popping open like a cartoon character. They were facing the *Centipede* cabinet now and Yosef seemed to recognize it, even in his dazed state.

"Here," Hank said, unsure whether he was about to continue speaking or not. He reapplied his grip to Yosef's long, greasy hair. It was tougher to get a hold of now with all the sweat and blood.

Hank brought his face down into the Plexiglas of the screen. Yosef's broken teeth and cheekbones didn't leave a scratch on the screen, instead his beard had soaked up enough blood that it formed a giant splotch.

Yosef had finally left his mark on *Centipede*.

Hank looked down at the play-area. *Centipede* was controlled using a trackball, that wouldn't do for what he had in mind. Turning Yosef around, Hank pointed him toward *Tapper* and flung him away. The barely conscious man's momentum sent him sailing, a WWF wrestler into a turnbuckle.

There was no more fight left in either of them now. Hank had resigned himself that the violence he was now inflicting on his friend, and the hate that caused it was now a part of him. Yosef had given up on everything but breathing, his intake of air a strained whistle, trying to suck oxygen through a cocktail straw.

Hank put one of the game's joysticks through Yosef's eye, burying it in his brain, then kicked the taller man's feet out from under him and left him hanging there, his skull bolted in place.

When it was done Hank took out his handkerchief and pocket knife.

He'd received the knife in the boy scouts, back when he used to see the outdoor world every once in a while. The handkerchief had belonged to his grandfather and he now used it to clean Yosef's blood off his glasses. Once he could see again, he took a look at his handiwork, folded the cloth up into a square and stuffed it back into his pocket. Then he sat with his back against the *Centipede* machine and sawed back and forth with the knife, opening his own throat.

CHAPTER 10

Kate had missed seeing the gate fall and sever Mr. Harmon's hands from his body, she'd been too busy texting her friend Donna.

HOLLY SHIT! SOME1 DEAD AT THE CAVE!!

When she looked back up, the gate was down and the group gathered there was scrambling to lift it. Dan was propping the glass doors open so they didn't have to hold them back to access the gate. The three boys had their bodies pressed against the metal partition, their fingers trying to find purchase on the smooth gate.

"It's locked in place," Jason Day screamed at Dan. "Do something!" Was that blood smeared across his white t-shirt?

Kate decided that it was time to leave the food counter and go help, or at least investigate so she could tell everyone what had happened: the cops, her friends, the news crew.

Crossing the arcade floor, she could smell barbeque. She worked at the lunch counter and knew that they didn't serve anything close to barbeque. Upon seeing Chris Murphy's burnt body, its legs crushed completely flat under the security gate, Kate felt both disgust and abject sadness. She should have been nicer to the kid. Her little brother went to school with him. She'd known his name ever since she'd started working at Funcave.

It was too late now.

Alongside the stumps of Chris's legs were a pair of hands, bleached white by blood loss. Her eyes ticked over, checking that Chris still had both his hands.

"Whose hands are those?" she said, her voice squeaky and the corners of her eyes burning with tears. The group turned to look at her, the same expression of confusion on all of their faces. They were trying to comprehend the incomprehensible, just like she was, even if she was a little later to the party than they were.

"Go get some towels or something," Cal Elliot said. Cal used to tell his friends that he hooked up with her one day after work, when Kate found out about the rumor she'd poured a jug of used fryer oil through the cracked window of his El Camino, ruining the front seat.

"Towels to do what? Chris is gone," she said.

"No, for the hands. We have to stop the blood or Mr. Harmon's going to die."

As if in answer, there was a groan from the other side of the gate. She looked at the hands again, noted the school ring wrapped around one pinky and the hair on the knuckles. They did belong to Eddie Harmon.

Kate raced off to grab some rags from the kitchen supply closet. There was a moment where she debated settling for a handful of napkins, but walking the extra few steps for the rags seemed like the right thing to do. Despite growing up telling everyone that she wanted to become a veterinarian when she was older, she didn't have any medical training. With or without the expertise, she could tell that Mr. Harmon had lost a lot of blood. Too much.

When she returned there was even more blood than she was expecting. The Asian girl, Tiffany, was kneeling and talking under the gate to Mr. Harmon.

"Hold on," she said under the door. Kate admired her, her bedside manner. "We're going to get this off you and the ambulance is already on its way."

Tiffany raised her head up and motioned to Kate. There was a speck of blood on her cheek from where she pushed it to the ground, the dark spot stood out on her white skin.

"Quick, give me those." The girl took the rags and spread them over Mr. Harmon's hands, then wedged the remainder under the door, like she was trying to lay down a towel to block a draft on a winter's night. The hands were unnaturally white, the consistency of wax candles. Kate should have brought ice, in case they needed to be reattached.

"Everyone listen," Dan said, he was trying to yell, but couldn't, it seemed to take him great effort to speak intelligibly under the best of circumstances. The three boys stopped struggling with the gate and listened. "The control panel is back in the office. One of you needs to run there, and use this key to try and raise the gate."

"I'll do it," Jason said. There was another person with leadership skills that made Kate feel ashamed for not helping sooner. If Mr. Harmon died, pausing to send that text would haunt her for the rest of her life.

"I'll follow you, but I won't be quick," Dan said, motioning at the right side of his body with his left hand. "There's a blinking red light on top and a keyhole that says 'open' on one side and 'closed' on the other. Turn it toward open."

"I figured," Jason said, then sprinted toward the back of the arcade.

As her eyes followed him, Kate realized that the metal partition between the arcade floor and the bowling alley had been lowered too.

"Are we trapped in here?" she asked aloud, but no one paid any attention to her, they were too excited by the gate opening. It was just an inch, but progress was progress.

"I've got it," Cal said, the veins of his arms popping as he fought against the gate. David rushed to help him, both of them getting their fingers to fit under the lip of the gate for the first time.

A moment later the whole room glowed blue and darkness descended upon them.

CHAPTER 11

Everything had gone so far, so fast.

Death. Death by the truckload. Uncontrollable, unexplainable, but all of it Robby's fault. Chris had poisoned him, turned his own network against him.

No, that wasn't it—he wasn't entirely blameless in the massacre. There was no Chris anymore, just like there hadn't really been a Robby Asaro since he'd taken a trip through the pizza oven in eighty-nine. There were just feelings and electricity, and now those feelings were predominately hate, pain and confusion.

He wished he could dissipate into nothing and take the memory of Chris Murphy with him. An object in motion would remain in motion, though. And besides, he felt so damn weak.

The hate dispersed throughout the arcade while Robby wasn't looking. Some of it had jumped into Hank McKenzie before anything could be done to stop it. Now the two most stalwart patrons of the arcade were dead, one with his blood and brains dashed all over *Tapper* and the other with his neck sawed in half by his own hand.

What he'd been trying to do with the gates was contain the situation, lock Chris Murphy's body out so matters didn't get any worse, but even that had backfired with deadly consequences. Breaking the gate hadn't been an accident, but he also didn't think that the results would be so bloody. At least, he thought that was true. It was impossible to be sure where the murderer ended and began, everything was so confusing right now.

Robby watched as Dan handed over the keys to Jason. They weren't calm, but they were taking action.

All of them, from Cal with his baggy shorts to Kate with her spray tan, had put aside their differences and were banding together to help. Robby was rooting for them, wanted to do something to help.

He spun the motor in the gate, thinking for a moment that he might be able to catch the latch and raise it back up, but he was only able to lift it less than an inch before it spun, nothing to hold on to.

The little victory had heartened the would-be rescuers, Cal and David got their fingers under the gate for a final push.

Please, Robby pleaded, he moved away from the motor to observe them from a better angle, hoping that in a few seconds he would watch them hold the gate triumphantly above their heads while everyone in the arcade scrambled out to the safety of the parking lot. *This place is damned, escape while you can.*

The lightning rippled across the beveled metal gate like blue spider webs.

Cal had placed one hand under the lip of the gate and the other hand flat against its side, so he was able to disentangle himself from the full force of the blast. David had squatted with both hands under, trying to pry the gate up the way an Olympic weightlifter would approach a dumbbell.

Cal shot back from the gate, the skin of his palms staying on the metal, blackening at crackling, all five fingers still distinguishable as the lightning dissipated.

Conversely, David was anchored in place by how low to the ground he was when the current had begun to flow. His knees pressed up into his chest, David was a ball of spasms. The muscles of his legs alternatively locked and loosened as the bolt traveled up and down the face of the door.

After a few seconds that seemed to drag on like minutes, the brilliance of the blue lightning faded and the room was plunged into darkness.

Robby, former king of the arcade, had now lost all control,

the pain of Chris Murphy was now able to travel wherever and do whatever it wanted.

After a minute of darkness, the only sound Cal's insensible cries of anguish and the breathless sobs of Dan, Tiffany, and Kate, the room was lit again by a soft orange glow.

David's shirt had quit smoking and burst into flames.

CHAPTER 12

As early as this morning, Dan looked forward to the sound of all of the games jumping to life. It was part of his daily ritual, throwing the circuit breakers located in the office and listening as the games, ten at a time, began to chirp their start-up music.

Now there was something unholy about the din. The girls used their sweatshirts to beat against the flames that had sprung up on David's back as all of the games rebooted themselves at once.

Shrugging through the pain that was eating up his right side, Boden bent down and cradled Cal's head.

"I saw it," Cal said, his eyes blood-shot to the point that there was no longer a speck of white to them. Dan guessed that right now the boy wasn't seeing much of anything, the electricity had boiled his eyeballs.

"It's all right," Dan said. He glanced over at the pair of hands that used to be attached to Eddie Harmon. The fingertips were black. If Eddie was going to survive having his hands lopped off, he certainly didn't make it through the blast.

"It's so angry," Cal said, his tongue sounding fat and dead in his mouth, Dan could relate. "It's everywhere." Cal shook his head from side to side, seeing something with his ruined eyes that Dan couldn't.

Boden shushed him.

Dan placed a hand on the boy's chest and beneath the thin undershirt it was hot to the touch. A loaf of white bread fresh from the oven, nearly too warm to hold. Dan didn't move his hand away, though, he kept it there until the boy's rapid heartbeat, overexerted with electricity and fear, cooled and went sluggish under his palm.

The boy died with his eyes open, drool running down his hot chin that evaporated but left a trail of slime behind.

Though he'd been in the presence of less live ones than an average man his age, Dan Boden had never seen a dead body.

Maybe he'd spent all those years in front of arcade machines and Excel spreadsheets of high scores because deep down he'd been frightened of when a day like this would come: when the mortality of other humans would be thrust into his face, forcing him to become an active participant in the world around him.

Not including himself, there were now three other people (that he knew of) in this arcade. All of them in harm's way. This was the first score he'd ever been faced with that mattered.

He looked away from Cal's body and saw that the girls had succeeded in putting out the fire. The air of the arcade carried a smoky haze now, the atmosphere filled with the stink of burning organic and inorganic matter now that the blood had boiled into the carpet.

One, two, Dan counted, looking to Tiffany and then to Kate. *Where's three?* Dan asked, remembering that he'd sent Jason to the office.

He wouldn't lose any more of them, couldn't. He needed to get the boy back with the group and find a way for everyone to make it through this, whatever *this* was.

Out in the night, the ambulance arrived, its siren blaring. Even though the gate was an inch above the ground, its material only a thin sheet of metal, help still sounded miles and hours away from those still alive in the arcade.

CHAPTER 13

Jason flicked the switch back and forth, but the lights in the office weren't coming back on.

He didn't smoke, but his mom did, so he'd grown used to carrying a Bic lighter. He wished one day he'd have a chance to light someone else's cigarette, a brunette from a black and white movie asking him for a light, but so far it had only been for his mom.

Rolling the starter with his thumb, the flame cast enough light in the room that he didn't knock his shins on anything, but that was about it. Everything was bathed in shadow and gloom and despite himself, he shivered.

Out on the arcade floor there was a loud crash that caused him to jump, his finger lifted up from the lighter and the office went black again. He froze in place.

Jason debated whether to run back to the front door to investigate or to continue trying to raise the gate. He had a responsibility to fulfill and time was wasting, flicking the lighter back on, he chose to tend to the gate.

The first wall panel he came to was the fuse box, although Dan hadn't told him to mess with it, Jason threw a few of the plastic breakers just to see if he could restore power to the office. Behind him, the laptop computer awoke from sleep mode, resuming a muted porno that had been paused on the desktop, but there was still no overhead light and the pink glow from the screen didn't add much to see by.

The gate control was simple and Jason found it quickly. It was like Dan had described: a blinking red LED and a rounded keyhole. Jason inserted the key into the slot, turned it to "open" and nothing happened.

He strained to listen if he could hear the clatter of the gate. There was silence in the room and muffled shouts from out front. He needed to get back out there and help.

There was another explosion of sound, this time from the laptop. The audio had clicked back on, the exaggerated sounds of coitus filling the room. Under such dire circumstances, seeing what he'd just seen, the glistening close-ups and wet smacking sounds of the porn turned Jason's stomach. He overlaid the images of Chris's crushed, broken legs to the sounds of the woman being entered on-screen. The combination was enough to turn him off porn for the rest of his life. Or at least the end of the week.

Looking at the computer screen, he could see that there was a window open behind the video that he hadn't noticed at first-glance. Moving his finger over the mouse, Jason clicked away from the pornography and brought the other window to full screen.

The window was divided into six separate squares of low-res black and white video feeds, arranged three by two across the screen. They were coming from the security cameras placed around Funcave and they were live. Jason wondered how that could be possible with no power. The laptop could be working off of its battery, but the modem and wireless router were powered off, he could see them stacked on top of the file cabinet next to the desk, their lights dead.

In one of the windows, Jason could see the first floor of the arcade, his view obscured by the placement of the camera and the darkness. It was clear that something new had gone wrong for the rest of his group, but he couldn't leave yet without glancing at the rest of the windows. The next four screens were empty, the power blinked back to the video games as he scanned through the images, offering a bit more light to see by.

On the final screen were two figures. This camera was placed upstairs, looking down over a section of the classic arcade. Jason rarely went up there, he found the emptiness of it kind of spooky, same as he did the old guys who hung out, pumping tokens into machines that were decades old.

Even with the poor image quality, Jason could tell that the men were dead. Their deaths were no accident, either. Neither of them had been struck by lightning or crushed by falling machinery: they'd been murdered.

On the monochrome screen, the puddles of blood that had formed under each man were inky black, their bodies motionless save for the occasional flicker of static.

The metal of the lighter was too hot to hold, so he let the flame die and upped the brightness on the monitor.

Jason stared at the image for a moment, trying to puzzle out who could have done this to the men. Every slasher movie he'd ever seen flashed before him, masked men dragging knives across throats, plunging joysticks through eyeballs. Had the killer rigged up the door to slam on the owner's hands? Was it a disgruntled employee out for revenge? The Phantom of Funcave?

The plot of his own movie unspooled before him like a blood-drenched episode of Scooby-Doo. The list of suspects limited by the people he'd met today that were still alive: Tiffany, Dan and Kate. His imagination only stopped pointing fingers when he realized that he was the only member of the group out on his own, alone. Never a good position to be in.

He began to turn away from the monitor, but a flicker of movement caught his attention before he could. One of the men was still alive. No, not alive, but moving.

The guy who'd been pinned to the *Tapper* machine moved his hand, his limp arm swinging back and forth at the shoulder. There was no way he could be alive, was there? Jason double-clicked, zooming in, making the feed larger but blurrier.

There was something coming out of the machine, working its way through the crevasses of the coin slot. The man's arm hadn't been moving, it was simply being displaced by whatever pale appendage was slithering out of the cabinet.

The long white worm glowed on the screen, wrapping around the corpse's legs, probing his pockets and coursing between his fingers, and all the thoughts that they might be the victims in a slasher movie evaporated from Jason's head: they were in a fucking monster movie.

His knuckles on the desk, Jason leaned forward to watch as this, a literal ghost in the machine, do its thing. The tendrils pulsed, looking like long elastic filaments, one moment ready to snap and the next fat slugs of phosphorescent light. There were two snakes now, with a third nosing its way out of the *Centipede* machine and investigating the gash at the second man's throat.

"What the fuck," Jason said aloud, the sound reminding him of how theatrical everything about this felt. *Game over, man. Game over*, he thought, the quote from *Aliens* taking on a new level of meaning in the arcade.

The tentacles stretching out of *Tapper* reached the dead guy's mouth and pushed their way inside, the ghostly white strand darkening with what Jason assumed was blood, feeding on the man like the proboscis of a giant mosquito.

That's when Jason felt it, the warm static hum touching the back of his hand. He pushed back from the desk, getting a good look at what had been going on as he stood mesmerized by the computer. Out of the sides of the laptop, oozing through the fan vents, the same appendages that were on-screen had materialized in the room with him. Even without the bloom of the black and white camera, they still emanated a pale green light as they writhed across the desktop, looking for Jason's hands.

He tried to imagine what they would have done if they'd gotten a hold of him before he noticed them. The back of his hand tingled from where it'd touched him and he wiped it on the back of his jeans, rubbing until his skin was raw.

Jason's frantic motions caught the attention of one of the strands and it rose up, extending itself out of the computer and coiling its base in order to push itself to eye-level with Jason.

The creature had no eyes, nose or mouth, none that Jason could see, but as he watched, it split itself into three, each tip peeling off of the trunk, the smaller strands becoming fingers on a hand. Jason pushed himself against the filing cabinet. He wanted to push the creature away but was afraid of letting it get a hold on him.

On the screen the white blob had overtaken the dead man's face, pushing into his ears and nostrils, dark with his blood. Jason could see himself falling victim to the same fate and looked for something to smack the snake away with.

The door behind him swung wide without warning, Dan moved faster than Jason had ever seen him, the two big steps he took into the room seeming more like hops. Jason moved out of his way and Dan used his good hand to bring his wrench down, not onto the tentacles themselves, but onto the laptop.

Jason could see that Dan was wearing heavy canvas gloves, both of which had been clipped to his tool belt alongside the wrench and his tape measure. The first hit caused a cloud of letters to fly up from the keyboard, the second made the screen go dark. With the third, the white arms lost their luminescence and dissolved into opaque puddles, dribbling over the edge of the desk.

After it was done, the only sound in the room was Dan Boden's panting, the older man was breathing so hard that he looked about ready to drop into convulsions. There was a satisfied look to him, though, his chest heaving in exertion but the corners of his mouth raised as he studied the busted computer, the melted tentacles.

"How do we get out of here?" Jason asked. Dan looked worried, the momentary victory of bashing in the computer forgotten.

"That's a really good question."

CHAPTER 14

Tiffany looked to Kate, asking "What do we do now?" without actually saying it.

She wrapped her arms around herself, a motion that should have instinctually brought comfort but instead only smeared the ashes of David's fire all over her forearms.

Boden's only instructions were to not touch anything and to try and warn the ambulance workers to do the same. The mechanic used his teeth to pull the thick glove down over his bad hand. Tiffany would have offered to help, but he was running off to the office before she could.

"It's the games." He'd said, the wisps of his balding hair upturned, making him look even crazier than the things he was yelling. "There's something in the electronics, or someone's controlling them. Don't go near them, don't even brush up against them. Just wait here while I go get your friend."

Their friend? Kate was not her friend, Tiffany had only ever exchanged words with the other girl while ordering curly fries. And Jason Day as the link between them? Tiffany liked Jason just fine, but it wasn't like they were hanging out every day after school. Something like this, people dead in strange and startling ways, pressed the survivors together, though. Maybe they were all friends now, the one thing they had in common being that they were alive and wanted to stay that way.

The ambulance rolled up and the only words Tiffany could make out from under the gate were: "holy shit," followed by the sound of liquid hitting concrete. If the first responders were puking because of what Eddie Harmon looked like, they should get a load of the two-and-three-quarters bodies that were still inside the arcade.

"Don't touch the gate!" Tiffany yelled, going to all fours so she could angle her voice out of the gap. Kate followed suit, the girl appeared dazed, but Tiffany could only imagine what her own expression must have looked like.

"It's electrified," Kate added. "Call the fire department and cut the power to the building."

That was good, Tiffany hadn't thought of that. Maybe she and Kate could be friends after all.

"Is everyone okay in there? Anyone hurt?" The voice sounded young, there was a pubescent crack on the word "hurt" that reminded Tiffany of her performance in the elementary school play. The ambulance worker was on the ground too, his voice close but still too far away to be of any real help.

Tiffany looked at Kate, they shared a moment, the three corpses around them providing an answer for the boy outside. "We're locked in here," Tiffany said. "There's four of us I think, everyone else is dead."

"My partner's on the radio with NHEC, fire trucks are on their way. Can you tell me your name?" he asked. They did. "If we can get the power switched off it's going to get very dark in there, you just need to stay calm, can you do that for me, girls?"

Tiffany looked to Kate, they both must have been thinking variations on the same idea. "Can you believe this asshole?"

"Yeah, we're good." Tiffany responded.

"Can you describe to me what it looks like in there? Is the power on?"

"It's dark, the only light is coming from the games."

"Did the lights go out after your friends got hurt?"

There was that word again, Tiffany wasn't friends with any of these people, and now never would be. "Yeah, the lights blew out after they were shocked."

"That's good, my partner and I are going to try to pry the shutters open, okay?"

"Don't!" Tiffany shouted. "We just told you it's electrified."

"We're going to be fine, we have gloves and I think that the first shock might have blown the power."

Kate spoke up. "I think you should wait."

"We want to get you out of there and help who we can as soon as possible, we'll be okay."

There was no more conversation after that, the polished metallic end of the pry bar dug under the space between the gate and the doorframe. A moment later it was joined by an identical wedge on the other end of the gate. The EMT they hadn't heard from yet, a female voice, gave a three count and the wedges lifted off the ground. The concrete grit on the other side of the doorway ground against the tools, but there was no movement from the gate beyond a slight ripple as they worked the heads of the bars back and forth.

Tiffany looked around the arcade, there was a crash somewhere in the office and she wondered if there was a window back there that Jason and Dan had decided to climb out of. No, they wouldn't leave them there alone, would they?

The metal gate groaned, the shutter rising a couple of centimeters.

"It's working," Kate said. Tiffany half-expected a streak of blue lightning, perfectly timed to coincide with Kate's optimism, but no bolt came. Instead the rescue workers readjusted their pry bars and continued attacking the gap.

"What are they doing?" Jason said, running out of the gloom, keeping his eyes glued to the arcade machines that he passed.

"They think the power's out. It's okay." Kate explained. "Look."

Dan followed Jason, his deterioration almost complete now. He was limping badly, but refused to reach out and use the machines to support himself. He really believed there was something wrong with the electronics.

"Stop," Dan yelled. "You need to back away."

"Calm down, sir," the squeaky voiced worker replied. "We've almost got it." In response to this, the gate opened another inch, far enough that Tiffany would have been able to stick her arm out and touch freedom if she weren't so concerned with losing it.

"Here, hold it up," the ambulance worker said, talking to his partner.

Tiffany was on her belly now, watching their boots as the one worker kneeled and gripped the edge of the door with both hands. He was wearing gloves, but they were hospital gloves and didn't seem anywhere near thick enough.

The gloves squeaked and stretched as the boy pulled at the gate, the shutter rising, miraculously and mercifully rising. Tiffany could feel the relief wash over her, could feel the shoulders of her fellow survivors, her new friends, getting a little lighter as well.

Then there was a choking sound from outside of the door and the gate slipped back down against the wedge. Tiffany watched as both pairs of boots were suddenly lifted off of the concrete, as if the rescue workers had discovered the secret of flight.

"Hello?" Kate said, there was no answer and Tiffany could see that the girl was blinking away tears.

"Oh shit." Jason said and turned to Dan. "It got them."

As if in response, something kicked against the outside of the gate, the metal segments buckling and then quieting. There were three more kicks, each one sounding progressively weaker, and then there was silence again from outside.

Dan sighed and then spoke. "There's a supply door in the back of the kitchen that gets used for food deliveries. Beyond jumping out the second story windows, that's the only way out I can think of. We need to try it now, though. Quickly."

"What got them?" Tiffany asked.

"Huh?" Dan groaned. He was busy tucking the sleeves of his shirt into the backs of the gloves, leaving no skin exposed. When he finished he squinted at the keys clipped to his belt. They were a mix of rounded keys that fit into arcade machines and regular ones that opened up the various supply closets and doors of Funcave. He wasn't going to answer her question, might not have even been aware that she had asked one.

"Jason, you said it got them, what got them?"

The boy looked embarrassed. He was no longer the class clown or the *Street Fighter* champion, but someone about to say a damning secret. "There's, like, bloodsucking ghost eels in the electronics."

Tiffany laughed a little bit, you could find levity in the strangest of places. She stopped laughing when her gaze shifted to movement beyond Jason, and she looked down near Kate's feet.

The bloodsucking ghost eels weren't quite as funny when you saw them slithering out of the prize door of a crane game, poised to grab your friend by the legs.

CHAPTER 15

It was getting crowded in here. The flood of memories was too much, Robby couldn't mediate them, they were a television with a million stations, the channel being flipped three times a second. Cal and David's memories weren't so bad, while Yosef and Hank's seemed to skew closer to the depressing side of things, but the real killer was still Chris's. The boy had lived eighteen years of torment, all of it he was now trying to inflict onto others.

Their deaths had awoken something in his network, his ectoplasm spooling around itself, pressing at the inside of his machines, doubling and tripling in mass with each death. There was something dangerous but intoxicating about it, after twenty years Robby felt like he had a physical presence in the world, that he was able to wiggle his toes or scratch his armpit, even if his armpit was on the second floor while his forefinger was in the office.

Dan Boden caving in the laptop didn't even sting, the computer was such a small part of him now that it were as if Dan had helped him clip a hangnail.

Maybe the introduction of Chris's hate into his system hadn't been a bad thing.

Hate was active, proactive, and that was something that Robby had lacked, all through his life and afterlife.

The ambulance drivers were the first murders that Robby didn't fight against. Not that he condoned them, but he did see how they might have been necessary. Their bodies were raw materials. And besides, Robby didn't know them. These people didn't even have names.

Of course, once they were dead, their mouths and sinuses filled with his membranous high-speed fiber optic cabling, then he knew their names. But by that point it was too late to save them.

The young man had been only twenty years old. He'd actually been in the Junior EMT program in high school, had only been out of school two years and was responsible for driving to scenes, saving lives. His name was Eric Kent. He had a second job at the pharmacy. The only bad thing he'd ever done was he'd once stolen a few tablets of Oxy for a girl he liked. She didn't sleep with him, no one had yet. No one ever would.

The woman was a bit older, her name was Suzanne Monetti. She looked too young to be a grandmother, only forty-two, but she was a grandmother nonetheless. Her daughter Gabby had made a mistake and brought Ruby Monetti into the world, five pounds two ounces. At least it seemed like a mistake at the time. Gabby wasn't the world's greatest mother, but Suzanne was trying her best to be the world's greatest grandma. Ruby had said "Meemaw" before she'd said anything else. That was two days ago.

Both of them tasted delicious, their bodies broken down and portioned out for the next phase of action. Robby decided that if Tiffany Park were going to die at all, she would die last and in such a way that Robby could rest assured that she would take her rightful place as the princess of the arcade.

It was the least he could do for her.

CHAPTER 16

Tiffany screamed her name, but Kate had no idea what she'd meant before it was too late and the things had wrapped themselves around her bare legs.

Their hold was slick, but firm.

She jumped, trying to push herself away from the machine, but the hands around her ankles held firm, tripping her. As she fell, Kate kept her hands out in front of her body, landing in a pool of congealed blood. Most of the blood had probably belonged to Mr. Harmon, but some could have been from the ambulance workers. She could still hear them outside, dead but their bones snapping, their bodies being reduced, dismembered.

Tiffany was the first to take action, bounding past Jason and grabbing Kate's forearms. The Asian girl was surprisingly strong for her size, sliding Kate's body further away from the machine, but not able to break the tentacles' grip.

The appendages were shooting out of the area reserved for picking up stuffed animals won while playing the game, the worms stretched and contracted in order to reel her in, ready to pull her up the half-foot wide chute.

There were tiny electric pulses up and down her legs, traveling to each hair follicle and exploding in her brain as images. In one flash she saw herself as a little doll, buttons for eyes and yarn for hair, nestled among the prizes in the game. It didn't seem all that bad, so she wasn't too alarmed when Tiffany lost her grip, the girl's fingers slipping on the dark blood.

Jason was at her feet now, stomping on the tentacles with all his might, but unable to sever the strands, only squishing them flat before they plumped up again in defiance.

Dan grabbed the boy by the shoulder. "No, stop. Help me move it." He motioned to the claw game.

She couldn't tell why everyone was so frantic, it didn't seem that bad. Just her foot was inside the door now, her shin wedged against the hard plastic flap. It should have hurt, but it didn't.

Jason pressed his shoulder to the side of the machine, pushing it against the carpet but not far enough for Dan's liking. Inside, the tiny crane jiggled, its claws opening and closing. It would be impossible to pick up anything with that thing, Kate thought. *What a rip-off.*

"Further! I can't reach it," Dan yelled.

The tentacles seemed to figure out what was going on and stopped trying to pull her up inside the machine, instead they slithered up her legs, wrapping around her torso to keep a strong hold.

Tiffany was standing now, trying to get all the leverage she could to pry Kate's foot out of the machine. Admittedly, Kate wasn't making it very easy for her, the hypnotic grip of the creature ordered her to make her arms go slack and Kate obeyed.

Tiffany was trying to help someone that didn't want to be saved.

Jason took a step back from the machine, wedged himself against the wall and pushed against it with both feet, moving it a few more inches before it couldn't go any further.

"I've got it" Dan said and finally Kate could understand what he was up to.

He was going to pull the plug connecting the machine to the wall.

"That's not going to work," Kate said, her voice giving no indication of panic.

As he unplugged the machine from the outlet she could feel it through the tentacles. There was a slight dip in strength, the electric hum not as strong as it had been, but they held firm. The only real consequence of unplugging the machine from the wall was that the arms advanced up her body, splitting and dividing, the more surface area of her body they stretched against, the more impossible her rescue seemed to become.

Objectively, she knew that this meant her own death, but she didn't much care, it didn't frighten her like it should.

"Look," Tiffany said, pointing up to the ceiling. There were more strands dipping down from the holes in the ceiling tiles, connecting the claw machine to the second floor, rerouting the power from the machines upstairs.

"Here," Jason said, making no indication as to his intensions but grabbing the wrench from Dan's belt before the older man could object. Kate watched as Dan's keys hit the ground, but it seemed like she was the only one who noticed.

Reaching up one hand to the top of the machine, Jason hoisted himself up so his head was close to brushing against the ceiling. He swung the wrench, breaking strands, weakening the power supply of the tendrils.

They were crawling up underneath her bra strap now, the arms ready to wrap around her neck. With less power the arms were more gelatinous now, leaving behind a cool viscous liquid as they moved along her body.

Tiffany kept pulling, but was careful not to let the goo touch her. That was good, Tiffany was a smart girl.

"Fuck," Jason yelled, his bare hand covered in strands of ectoplasm, the fingers were more intent on wresting the weapon from his fist than they were with reeling him in and devouring him.

Jason allowed himself to fall back, the wrench still stuck in the thickening mass of tentacles connecting the first floor to the second floor like oversized cobwebs.

The hands were at her neck now and she could feel pinpricks in her cheeks as the chords tightened and deprived her of oxygen. Her vision clouded as blood vessels began to burst.

"No," Tiffany said, sobbing. Jason had his hands on hers now, guiding them away from Kate's body, away from the tendrils that were now coiled around every square inch of her.

There was pain now, finally. After a burst of red, there was a sharp tug at her knee and Kate could no longer feel her toes.

She watched as her sneaker worked its way up the chute and was deposited on top of the plush Angry Birds and knock-off Beanie Babies that lined the inside of the glass case. Her foot was still inside the shoe, the entire thing webbed in strands of filament, no longer pale green but dark red, feeding on the wound.

The last thing she was aware of as herself, was the tendrils sweeping the floor under the machine, grabbing onto the keys and dragging them out of Dan's sight.

The worms filled her nose, began feeding on her memories and suddenly Kate was everywhere and nowhere. One with the arcade.

CHAPTER 17

Kate was in pieces, stacked with the stuffed animals inside the glass case of the claw game. But that wasn't the worst part, because inside with her, resting between her pelvis and her head, was Boden's ring of keys, covered in green-white filament.

It were as though the creature, fungus, whatever, was taunting him. *You had a way out, but now I've taken it from you. Why don't you put a few tokens in the machine and see if you can fish it out?*

Jason and Tiffany were huddled together, as far from the arcade machines as they could get. Both of them were crying. There was no machismo to Jason anymore, none of the save-the-day gusto he'd shown when he'd taken the wrench from Dan's belt and started swinging away. Now there was just a scared boy who'd just seen a girl divided into twenty different parts. If anything, Tiffany was the one consoling him, her hand making small circles on his back.

There were no hugs for Dan Boden, the man who stood apart, not just in age or lifestyle, but because Dan knew what he was going to do next. Dan was ready for action.

He walked over to them, dragging his right foot. It was too much trouble to lift it up at this point. Whispering was near impossible with his mouth the way it was, but he tried anyway. If this thing could hear, it may be able to understand what he was saying and he couldn't risk that.

"When I get those keys," Dan said, not talking to Jason or Tiffany but right in the middle of them, because it was of equal importance that they both understood. "I'm going to do my best and clean them off before I toss them to you. When you have them, you run. You don't go anywhere else but straight to the kitchen and out the door."

"You can't, you saw what it did to her," Tiffany said, but her voice told him that she understood that he had to make the attempt.

Jason took a breath and stared down at his own hand before offering his opinion. Moments ago that hand had been coated in phosphorescent sputum. The smell of the stuff was thick in the air. "If it touches you, it tells you things. Don't listen to it."

Dan didn't quite understand what the kid meant, but he nodded like he did.

"We don't even know that we need them, the door might not be locked." Tiffany offered her theory weakly, as if she knew that the door locked automatically, that there were only two keys to it because it was only used once every two weeks for deliveries. She didn't possess that knowledge, but Dan did. The other key was in Eddie Harmon's pocket on the other side of the gate.

"The key is one of the silver ones, I think," Dan said. All of them were silver, so it may well have been an attempt at humor, but he didn't mean it that way. "Do you understand?"

Tiffany and Jason's faces were tearstained, the girl's porcelain complexion gone, subsumed by red.

"That a yes?" he asked, no longer even attempting to whisper.

They both echoed a reluctant yes.

"Good."

Walking over to the gate, Dan reached down and grabbed the pry bar that lay half in and half out of the arcade, the wedged end was facing in, so it was easy to slide the handle under the gate, the metal on metal scrape filling the air with noise. Once completely under, the gate slammed closed, cutting off the sliver of light from the parking lot lamps, making it that much darker inside.

The bar was heavy, had to be for the job it was intended to do: save lives.

Dan held the curved end with his left hand, forcing his paralyzed right hand to curl around the base and hold the bar steady. He looked up at the ceiling, the area above the claw machine was heavy with amorphous stalactites (or was it stalagmites?). In the darkness of the arcade, their pale points changed color as they reflected the light from the games below. The tentacles moved gently, dancing in a wind that wasn't there as they changed from pink to orange to lime green.

There was a delicate jellyfish beauty to them until Dan looked down at the mess they had made of Kate, a girl whose only sin was sticking her bubblegum under the lunch counter.

Dan hefted the metal bar over his shoulder and brought it down on the glass of the claw machine. The pane shattered at the top, exploding outwards as the spongy contents poured out like he'd struck a fish tank. They'd been waiting for him, coiled and ready to strike when he broke the glass. He didn't even follow through, just dropped the bar and forced his hand forward, grabbing at the place where the keys had been, before the glass had been removed and the contents of the machine had begun to shift.

He needed to keep his attention on the sprawling mass in front of him, but he couldn't help but sense Jason and Tiffany start to move, to help him.

"Stay back, don't come over here!"

Dan leaned into the machine, broken glass crunched under his heels. He could feel the tentacles already gripping at his ankles and was thankful that he was wearing dress socks that went up to his knees.

A mass of smaller tendrils were twisting and combining to his right, ready to lash out at his bad side. He ignored them and grabbed for the keys again. Instead of pulling back, this time they keys dove deeper into the pool of prizes. Trying to dismiss the fact that many of the items he was pushing out of the way used to be Kate's vital organs, Dan dug deeper into the pit. He was bobbing for apples in the sink of a butcher's shop, the smell burned past his nose hair.

The tentacles grabbed his right forearm and began working the glove off of his paralyzed hand. He could feel the attack, the attempt to probe his mind, but it was a dull sensation, far from mind control. Dan could taste the electricity on the back of his tongue, like licking a nine-volt. *That the best you got?* He thought, and somewhere too far away to be understood, he thought he could hear an answer.

With his good hand he began tossing the contents of the bin over his shoulder, still searching for the keys. Under his belly he could feel the jagged glass of the case grinding into his stomach. Leaning over the lip of the trough had been a bad idea, but it was the only way. Grunting through the pain, he moved a gore-drenched green pig and found them, webbed into the corner of the machine.

The slime that glued them in place was strong, Dan's joints—his good ones—howled their unhappiness. He pulled, lifting the keys up becoming easier as soon as the first few strands had been broken. The material snapped free with a Velcro sound.

"Got them," Dan said.

In his mind, this had always been a one-way trip. When he decided to get the keys, he was deciding to sacrifice himself for the good of the group, for the kids, but now that he had them and was relatively unharmed, he felt hope kindle inside him.

It was trying to turn his body around that tossed a blanket over that hope, smothering it. He'd been so intent on the keys that he hadn't realized that he was cemented in place, the large cobbling of tentacles having completely overtaken his left arm and shoulder.

"Take them," Dan said, "but try not to touch it." He was drooling now, bent backwards as far as his body would let him. He was sweating in his clothes and could feel the blood rushing to his head. In his imagination he could see the shunt in his brain, the levees getting ready to break, letting a torrent of blood flood his mind. This time the stroke would kill him, he was sure of it.

The fingers were crawling up his neck now, the buzzing sensation much more powerful as the strands reached flesh that still had feeling. Now he knew why Kate had surrendered so easily:

It was wonderful.

He could see them all, real as day, and they were all waiting for him. He walked up to the table and took a seat. Hank and Yosef, his two remaining friends were there, along with Funcave's old chef, Robby. Jeez, he hadn't thought about Robby in ages.

"Welcome," Robby said, placing a pizza box down on the table Dan and his friends were seated around. The pizza was meatball and green peppers, the kind of food Dan was supposed to avoid nowadays, but it smelled so good. His mouth watered and he lifted up a slice.

Using his right hand, he was surprised to find that it no longer hurt to move his fingers. In fact, his fingers seemed younger.

He looked back up at Hank and Yosef. Hank's glasses weren't so thick and the end of his nose was no longer marked with red veins. Yosef's beard was only a peachfuzz mustache clinging to his upper lip. They were teenagers again and so was Dan Boden.

"So what do you want to play after we eat?" Hank asked, his smile highlighting something that Dan had forgotten about: Hank had freckles! Wasn't that amazing? Noticing something that small and having it flood you with emotion all these years later.

"You've got to let them go!" a black kid yelled from the arcade floor, intruding in Dan's meal with his friends. Dan didn't begrudge him though: everyone should be allowed to have a good time at the arcade.

Suddenly there was a bottle of Coke in his left hand, the green glass smooth and cool against his palm. It was moist and good and he gripped it tight. The slice of pizza folded in his right hand and the Coca-Cola in his left, Dan spoke to Hank again.

"What did you ask?"

"What's on the agenda after pizza? They just got that new *Tron* game in, I want to check it out, don't you Yosef?"

Yosef probably wanted to play *Centipede*, Dan thought to himself. Classic Yosef.

"Open your hand!"

Did the kid mean him? Why should he?

"Please, Dan!"

Well, he did use the magic word.

Dan set the bottle down on the table and opened his fist, whipping the condensation on the red, checkered tablecloth.

"Why did you do that, Dan?" A voice asked. There was a new kid at the table with them. That was okay, but Dan had wished he'd asked permission to join them. It was the kid from the arcade earlier, the one who dressed in black and said cruel things. Had all that been today? It was getting hard to remember what day it was. What year.

"You shouldn't have done that," Chris Murphy said.

As he said that the room darkened, the table disappeared and the bottle dropped to the ground, breaking into a million pieces.

When Chris Murphy was around, the arcade ceased being wonderful.

Dan awoke from his daydream just long enough to watch himself be torn in half.

CHAPTER 18

Closing off the kitchen door had been tricky, but Robby had been able to manage it.

There were very few electronics back in the kitchen beside the fryers and those were too far away from the door to be of much use. The door was analog and there was no alarm connected to it, so there was no waypoint for him to travel to and take control of. What he did instead was use the nearest wall outlet, materializing three strands of ectoplasm and squeezing them out of the socket. Even with all the nourishment from the EMTs, Kate and, now, Dan Boden, pushing a new armature out of the wall was taxing. Worse yet were the boxes stacked in front of the outlet that he had to push over. He was tired and it felt as if he were rolling a tube of toothpaste, trying to get the last drops of energy out of it so he could finally have some clean teeth.

Using the doorframe for stability, Robby sent the rope up to the keyhole, flattening the end out and filling the mechanism of the door with plasma. Even if Jason was able to wrestle the pry bar from him, the heavy steel door wasn't going anywhere unless they could unlock it.

Funcave was now completely secure.

Hank and Yosef were now digested and Robby had been sure to hide any items he couldn't breakdown (Hank's glasses or Yosef's metal fillings, for instance) where no rescue workers could find them. Suzanne, Eddie, and the Kent boy were well on their way to disappeared and Robby hoped to have them gone by the time the fire department arrived. He didn't need any more witnesses.

Nothing was perfect, there were still some stained bits of carpet and the broken crane machine, but Robby wouldn't be suspected of the crimes committed here tonight. He didn't give much thought to what explanation the police would give it, but he was sure that it would be terrestrial. Besides, once tonight was over nobody would hear from Robby Asaro ever again. He'd be content. He already felt Chris's hate subsiding, once all this was done, he would be back in control.

The flickering of memories had stopped now. Either that or he'd learned to ignore it. He knew every secret these people ever kept, so in a way he was closer to them than their parents, lovers or spouses. He was giddy with anticipation to know everything about Tiffany Park, anxious that he would be disappointed but sure that he wouldn't.

But first things first: he had to make sure that neither Jason nor Tiffany were around to tell anyone what really happened.

CHAPTER 19

Jason had taken back his sweatshirt to wipe the slime off of the keys. Tiffany didn't need it anyway, she'd dried off and now it had gotten hot in the arcade.

All the machines were radiating heat, she wondered if they had always been like that or that now since the arcade was blocked off from the bowling alley the heat was exacerbated. She knew that the real answer was probably worse, that inside each machine the circuits were smothered with those things, waiting to lash out at her and tear them apart. That's why they were running hot.

"There are six silver ones," Jason said, dropping the sweatshirt to the ground as he walked and leaving it there. He fanned the keys out in her direction. "Pick one," he said.

She wanted to tell him to choose, that she didn't want to be responsible for guessing wrong and having them stuck here any longer than they had to be. She thought of Dan, his right side being torn from his body from his shoulder down, the pathetic little hop that his good half had done before it flopped over, dead, the blood pouring out of him.

"That one," she said, pointing to a key. She tried to choose the shiniest among them, hoping that the glint was some sort of divine signal, even though she didn't believe in God. She didn't believe in ghost octopi either, so stranger things had happened.

They passed the ticket redemption counter, but Tiffany hardly looked in that direction, she kept her eyes glued to the Skee-Ball. In her mind, she watched as tentacles rose up out of the holes, pelting the wooden balls at her and Jason, beating them to death as tickets streamed out of the slot, rewarding every hit. *The arcade is striking back*, she thought, *not even the claw game is safe.*

She could breathe easier when they had passed the row of machines. Even though the air was usually clogged with fried food, it smelled cleaner in this section of the building. It were as if the infection that had taken hold of the machines hadn't reached this far, like there was still a chance to save Funcave's soul.

They ducked under the lunch counter and walked through the doorway into the darkness of the kitchen. Without the arcade machines surrounding them, the air was cooler and Tiffany's claustrophobia dissipated, but there was no light to see by.

She took Jason's hand, instinctually, no longer thinking in boy/girl terms, just looking for another human being in the void.

"Fuck," Jason gasped, but he'd only bumped into a cardboard box on the floor, the sudden obstacle causing him to jerk back. The keys jingled somewhere ahead of her and Jason struck up a flame, the small Bic lighter he carried forming shadows of orange and black in the room.

The floor at their feet was covered in white and red napkins, the Funcave insignia emblazoned on each. Stacks of the napkins rested inside the box to her right.

Behind the boxes, she could see the door. There was no crack at the bottom, no way to tell whether or not the real world lay on the other side. The lack of proof made it that much harder to believe that this was the end. That escape would be this easy.

"Hold this for me," Jason said and handed her the lighter. She'd let it go out for a second, but flicked it on again. The metal of the starter burnt her thumb, but she didn't care.

Jason held the key up to the light.

He gave her hand a squeeze. "Here we go," he said. She wished he would stop talking, stop building it up. If you didn't act like there was a chance it wasn't going to work, then success seemed more likely.

There was a moment where it didn't seem like the key was going to fit, but then it began to slide home. The metallic clatter as the grooves of the key ran over the tumblers was one of the sweetest sounds Tiffany had ever heard.

"Just turn it already," she shouted.

"I'm trying," Jason said and she could see that he was telling the truth, the veins on his hand and forearm stood out as he struggled to turn the key in the lock.

Tiffany opened her mouth to say something, but she didn't know what. Instead of words, her mouth was spattered with the coppery taste of blood and sweat as Jason's face seemed to cave inward.

No.

The tentacle had hidden itself inside the space between the door and the frame, made itself paper thin and struck while neither of them had been looking. Instead of the gentle slathering in ooze that the others had undergone, this time there was only one appendage. It had reduced itself to the size of a pencil, dense and sharp at the end, and shot into Jason's nostril, looping back out his tear duct.

Tiffany watched for one horrifying moment as Jason's eye rolled backward, displaced by the writhing mass that had wrapped itself around his cheekbone. The tentacle pulled and Tiffany heard the snap of bone.

Too late, she pressed the flame to the strand and watched as the rope melted with a hiss. It had been so easy to break the filament with flame, why hadn't they tried it earlier? His tether to the wall broken, Jason dropped to the ground, dead.

The broken end of the thing that was still connected to the door lashed out, but not fast enough to catch her. She pressed herself flat against the boxes behind her, tripping and landing hard, the thin layer of napkins doing little to cushion the tile floor of the kitchen. In the struggle, the flame was extinguished again, she was momentarily in darkness, half expecting something to slither up her leg and end it before she could regain her sight.

Burning her thumb again, she rolled the starter, the flame refusing to appear the first attempt but jumping to life with the second.

The tentacle wasn't chasing her down, but instead had wrapped itself around the doorknob. She watched as it flexed, the key still in the knob, the rest of the keys wobbling on the ring below. There was a dull snap and the key ring dropped to the floor, bouncing off of Jason's lifeless chest.

The creature had broken the key off inside the lock.

Hopelessness, ashy and bitter, filled Tiffany Park.

"Why are you doing this?" she screamed, first at the tentacle itself, then at the room around her, sensing that she was surrounded.

The hopelessness peaked and then receded, replaced instead with anger. It was a nihilistic, proactive anger. She'd found the thing's weakness too late to save her friends, probably to save herself, but she would not go quietly.

The knuckle of her thumb ached, but she pressed down on the lighter harder, ignoring the heat. With her free hand she gathered up a bundle of napkins and held them over the flame. They smoked and sparked, before lighting up the room in a brilliant amber glow. The flame ate them up before she could let them go, embers swirled at her feet but were not enough to ignite the napkins on the floor.

She tried again, taking a bigger handful this time, then laying them down against one of the boxes.

"Fuck you," she yelled, to no one but the empty room. She filled her pockets with napkins and when those were full, she stuffed the waistband of her jeans.

The flames in the kitchen were tall now, but she couldn't trust them to do the job. Exiting the kitchen, she ducked under the lunch counter and started for the ticket redemption area. She cut herself breaking the display case with her shoulder, but couldn't tell how badly. She set fire to a row of stuffed animals, the cheap plush material smelled awful as it burned. The scent was a mix of plastic chemicals and bleached paper but it was still better than the fungal stink of the arcade.

She grabbed a half-engulfed bear by its neck and tossed it over to one of the Skee-Ball lanes. Out of the ball door, a tentacle emerged, touched the flames, and immediately fizzled.

For the first time in a long time, Tiffany wished that she could see herself. If only she was one of those girls that carried a compact in her pocket, she'd be able to see her wild pyromaniac hair, the look of destructive joy that had curled her grief-stricken mouth into something like a smile.

At the start of the arcade floor, she bent, found a section of frayed carpet and pulled it up, the fabric ripping easily. Around her the machines chirped, their volume cranked and the radio switched off. The bells and 8-bit music no longer sounded cheerful, but frantic. If it were a person, she'd be burning the arcade alive and loving it.

The carpet ignited and she used the flame to start up a wad of napkins, now soggy from the sweat of her belly. She tucked the sputtering mound of paper under *Mortal Kombat*, the demo screen showing a fight between Scorpion and Johnny Cage.

"Finish him!" the game cried, as if it understood irony. It took a moment but the particle board of the machinery went up.

From the coin door of *Street Fighter Alpha*, from where she hadn't been watching, an appendage had snaked up her Vans, yanking her foot out from under her. It had her now, but she whipped her foot into the flames, not feeling the heat, and watched as the arm evaporated.

The blast had been strong enough to soften the soles of her shoes, but it didn't hurt. The fire had cleansed her. That was all.

She lit up five more machines before she ran out of napkins. The room was thick with smoke, so she ducked down and crawled to the gate. There were no sirens yet, so much for the fire trucks that a small part of her brain still believed would rescue her.

Tiffany sat with her back to the front wall, the concrete cool against her spine. There she waited, but not for long. Above her, through the dense smoke, she could see movement.

In all the excitement she'd forgotten about the classic arcade. The ceiling writhed, the tentacles a frantic mass of movement. They knew that this was the end, but they were going to drop down upon her before they burned up.

"I killed you," she said, looking up as they made their tentative decent, the boiling air causing them to drip like melting icicles. The heat was destroying them, but not fast enough.

It had a hold of her, she couldn't fight it anymore. Even though she could feel its fear, its anguish at the arcade cabinets burning, it wasn't angry with her. To Tiffany's surprise it was trying to reassure her, let her know that she was going to be safe. If only she'd just trust it.

You can live on. Please. You'll be royalty.

Maybe it was mind control, but she believed it. She called the presence by its name—Robby—and gave herself over to it, following it into oblivion as the fire raged around her.

EPILOGUE

George Allen's home arcade was completely bitching, but it was not yet complete.

He'd lain down carpeting, bought a dehumidifier, and had five of his six top games already refurbished and installed, but there was still something missing.

This project had all started when he'd picked up a run down Neo Geo cabinet at a garage sale. He hadn't planned to start collecting, it had just happened. A few clicks around on the internet and he'd landed on a series of videos telling him how to get the machine looking and playing like new.

George was now a hobbyist. Well, he was more than that really. In a day and age where most arcades were closed, most games being sent to the landfill, George was helping to preserve cultural artifacts. At least, that's what he'd told his wife when she'd snooped around in his credit card statements.

One *Burger Time*, a *Sinistar* and a *Black Knight* pinball machine later and his dream arcade was nearly complete. It had to be, he was running out of room. There was only one machine he hadn't tracked down yet: *Ms. Pac-Man*.

It was not a hard machine to find by any means. But he could never land on one in the right condition for the right price. The problem he was finding was that most of the machines for sale were reproductions that included *Galaga* in the same cabinet. No offense to *Galaga*, but George wanted an original.

His problem was solved when he stumbled on a Craigslist post about an estate auction being held at a burned-down arcade. He drove up to New Hampshire, paid his hundred bucks and came back home with a slightly-charred (but original) *Ms. Pac-Man* tied down to the bed of his truck.

Once he'd scrubbed off some of the carbon scoring and touched up the paint on the corners of the machine, he drilled open the coin door (the keys hadn't been included in the auction) and poked around. Aside from a moist, fishy smell the insides of the machine looked pristine. Before he dug any deeper and opened the back of the machine up, he decided to try plugging it in. The colors on screen were bright and vibrant, the sounds were note perfect and the controls were slick and responsive.

He'd gotten a great deal and probably wouldn't have to check the tube for a year or more.

§

Behind the screen, beyond where George Allen had thought to check, something stirred. The movement was strained and weak from the journey across two states, but the spongy material caked behind the marquee had held firm. In the days after being re-introduced to a new arcade, the spark of ideas and electricity allowed itself to feel stronger, until it had grown into a physical manifestation of that strength.

Inside of George Allen's *Ms. Pac-Man* machine, there were two human hearts beating as one. One the heart of a princess, the other the heart of a God.

No, George Allen's home arcade wasn't Funcave, but it was a start.

Zero Lives Remaining is over, but read on for a special bonus story...

STARTING EARLY

The feeling peaked at age twelve and it's been a case of diminishing returns every year since.

I still chase the high, though.

And I begin to chase it early in the season.

The checkout girl is more dead-eyed than usual as she swipes the barcodes on my bags of candy corn and individually wrapped Reese's.

Supermarkets are one of the first places to start putting out their Halloween supplies, beginning with candy. Pharmacies are a close second, and they usually put out both decorations and candy at the same time.

All that's true unless you count party stores, a few of which keep a dedicated costume and decorations aisle year-round.

There's a Party City not far from where I live, but I haven't owned a functioning car in years, and the bus lines going out there don't seem worth the effort. So I settle for the supermarket, at least until the CVS up the block starts putting out their masks, window clings, and singing candy bowls.

It's the first week in September though, and supposed to go up to 93 degrees by tomorrow afternoon. Fall's not here yet; I have time.

"Do you have a discount card?" the girl asks.

She sees me multiple times a week and asks me this same question every time I'm in her lane.

It does wonders for my self-esteem to be remembered.

"No, but can you run one for me?" I respond. This is what I always say, but none of the candy was marked as discount, so the total is the same.

I pay. As the girl hands me back my change, I notice that she, too, is wearing chipped nail polish, a similar shade to mine.

I wonder how old she is. High school?

In a couple of decades, her own dead-eyed checkout girl won't recognize her either.

I leave the store, candy in hand. It's all I've purchased on this trip, but it's not like that's all I eat. I did my shopping on Monday and have plenty of leftovers from a casserole I made last night.

The walk home doesn't take long but I do have to traverse a long stretch of road that has no sidewalk. Kids in a Jeep yell something at me as they pass and I flinch, not at the words but from how close the car comes.

I've been called worse and today is a good day.

Cecily waits for me on the second floor landing. She's been loitering outside the door to my apartment, but she stares down at her phone, pretending to be busy.

What does a ten-year-old need with an iPhone? And how can her parents afford it? I've asked these questions—internally—several times, but I'm never comfortable enough around the girl to ask.

"Miss Maggie," she says, not really yelling my name, but sounding happy to see me as I begin to ford the steps.

She runs down to "help" me with my bag, but she knows I don't need the help. And she wants to secure some of the candy for herself.

"Are we unpacking the village today?" she asks.

Yes. Yes we are. Somewhere she must have a calendar with these dates. Together we've decided on a schedule for preparing different elements of my Halloween display.

I don't live in a large apartment, but it has a spare room and I've utilized that space the best I can to store my collection without looking like an insane hoarder. In that room, floor-to-ceiling, I've stacked orange and black plastic Rubbermaid bins. Each one is a little over knee-high and can hold a surprising amount.

"Yes, and you can help, but you have to be very careful," I say, digging in my purse for the keys.

"I got it," Cecily says, pinching the spare key I've given her from her necklace. It's supposed to only be for emergencies, but there's been times where I've suspected Cecily has been in my apartment without me. At least, that's what I would have done if I were her age.

We enter, I prepare a bowl for the candy, slice both bags open and pour them in.

Cecily uses her phone to bring up a playlist she's prepared for the next two months. It starts with "The Monster Mash" and then moves to newer songs I'm not a huge fan of, but they stay within the seasonal theme and Cecily enjoys them.

It will take us an hour or two, but once we get the village set up, the coffee table in the living room will be unusable for the rest of the season.

Cecily munches candy corn and follows me underfoot as I go through the boxes in the spare room, looking for the one labeled "Spookyville".

That's the name I've given to the collectable ceramic town I've accrued over the last decade. Christmas villages have been a staple among *those* collectors for ages, so it's only fair that the Halloween industry caught up in recent years.

"Maybe it's in one of these," Cecily says, pressing a finger against one of the three containers that don't match the storage room's black and orange color scheme.

The blue bins are similar in shape but I've lined them up against the far wall. Then I've stacked heavier Halloween bins on top to prevent a curious Cecily from opening them.

"No, those are just old clothes, honey." She's been told this several times.

"Here it is," I say, attempting to redirect my young charge's attention. I begin to pick up the box, then pause and look to the little girl. "Wait. When do you have to be home? Maybe we shouldn't start this project now."

"Missssss Maggie!" Cecily says, impatient and crossing her arms.

Her huff is cute, but I think she knows that I'm kidding.

If Cecily's mother knows or cares where the girl spends most of her after-school time, I certainly haven't heard about it. Perhaps she's afraid that if she talks to me about it, I'll try to negotiate a pay-rate for all the free babysitting I'm providing.

We clear a space and begin unpacking the village. I've kept the houses in their original packaging where possible and wrapped all of the loose accessories in paper towels to keep the delicate pieces safe.

The smell of the old paper towels is one of those unexpected nostalgia triggers. I unroll a tiny polyresin Frankenstein's monster and the moment the slightly-mildewed wood-pulp reaches my nose I get a hit of the feeling.

It's the feeling I first remember having in the mid-seventies, watching Morticia Addams in re-runs and wanting my very own Lurch.

It's a feeling that I'd tried to foster at the dawn of the internet era by contributing to early message boards on the subject and connecting with fellow collectors. That was the first time I found out there were people just like me all around the country.

That was a while ago, but I still put pictures of my displays up on my Facebook. The loss of anonymity on the internet has turned me off the community, though. I used to like knowing nothing about my friends beyond their screen name. The bloom is off the rose now that I can click on any friend's profile and see that—during the other ten months of the year—their life is just as depressing as mine.

"I like this one," Cecily says, holding up the town's florist, which has giant Venus fly traps painted behind its windows and thorns growing up its brick front.

Cecily is careful, like I've requested, but she's still only a child and my stomach drops every time it looks like she may let something slide through her fingers and onto the thin carpet of my living room.

"I like it too," I say, although it's one of my least favorites. It's a newer piece and the manufacturer has changed the scale of every building they've released since 2011. Which means the florist and the apothecary don't look right when placed next to the haunted house and the mausoleum.

"I wish you had a butcher shop." Cecily says. "With severed arms in buckets and chainsaws. *That* would be scary. "

Cecily has been saying things like this for the past few weeks, in the build up to the season. I think she wants me to take her more seriously. Or she's been browsing different websites and getting a wildly divergent definition of what the season's about than I had when I was her age. It's supposed to be fun, not grim.

"That wouldn't really fit," I say, unrolling a witch seated side-saddle on her broom. "She doesn't look like she would shop there to me." I hold up the witch so Cecily can inspect her pointed hat and the purple trim of her cape.

"Sure she would," Cecily says, "witches eat children. She would buy candy from the candy store," she points at the small sweets shop and continues, "to fatten the kids up and then she would bring them to the butcher to be slaughtered."

It's so grotesque I have to laugh to cover up the shiver from the word slaughter. It doesn't strike me as the kind of word a girl Cecily's age should be using yet.

I realize I'm both repulsed by her dark thoughts and don't want her to grow up too fast.

"No, that's not what this witch does at all," I say, not meaning to snap but doing it anyway. Cecily offers no rebuttal, only looks down at her hands.

We don't speak as we finish the rest of the unpacking; after a period of silence, Cecily hums along with her music.

Once the mood has lightened, I let some candy corn dissolve in my mouth. It's probably worse for my teeth, eating them this way, but they're the first I've had all year and the sweetness is a time-release drip of that Halloween feeling. In a week they'll lose their novelty, if I eat them every day, so I resolve to try not to do that.

We finish putting the town together and I plug in all the lighted house pieces into a surge protector. Then we turn off the living room lights and watch the town glow for a minute before Cecily looks at her phone and says she has to be home for dinner.

I spend the rest of the night staring in the windows of the town and fall asleep on the couch.

When I wake, it's already too late to take a shower before heading in to work.

I work part-time. Not that I'm shifting toward retirement, but because I have very few needs. I have a little saved up for rent and don't mind eating microwave noodles for two out of three of my daily meals.

My only real expense is my collection, and even that I've cooled on in recent years. There's not much that excites me anymore; I still buy, but I buy out of obligation and habit.

The eight-twenty bus is pulling away as I walk up to the stop, so I end up punching in late.

I'm an attendant at the Babylon train station. When I first took the position, I feared it would be too much customer interaction for me, but it turns out that I barely have to speak. There's an inch and a half of Plexiglas between me and the commuters and most know what kind of ticket they need when they approach the counter. I only need to hold down the intercom button and press a few keys on my computer.

Today I work six hours and arrive back home a little after three-thirty.

Cecily is not on the landing when I return, which is surprising but maybe the awkwardness of me losing my temper with her last night has kept her away.

I put my key in the lock, turn the knob, and am dismayed to see that I haven't unlocked the door, but locked it.

My mind immediately goes to a burglary and my heart flutters.

Not that I have much to steal, but I've been robbed before and the thieves were not gentle with my collectables.

Turning the key again, the door swings open and I peer into the hallway that opens onto my living room. It's darker than it should be and I can't even see the end of the hallway. Behind me the sun is bright and should be pushing through the blinds.

"Hello?" I ask into the gloom. At first there's no response, and then I hear it.

The sound of a heartbeat.

It's not my own—I'm not that scared—but I do recognize it. The heartbeat's from the beginning of a novelty sound effects CD I use to set the mood for my collection. But I don't usually play it until the second week of October, when there's a reason for those sounds to be pouring out my open windows. I usually put it on when I've taken the batteries out of the smoke detectors and turned on my fog machine for the first time.

No thief would put "Creepy Sounds for your Haunted House Vol. 2" on before leaving the scene of a crime.

"Cecily," I say into the darkness, stepping over the threshold. I try not to let into my voice how upset I am to have my privacy invaded like this.

I never should have made her that key.

I close the door behind me and the hallway goes dark, just a faint glow from the living room. She hasn't just closed the blinds, she's pulled the blackout shades shut.

There's the sound of rattling chains and the moan of a ghost, signaling the CD is transitioning to a new soundscape.

"Cecily, you're not supposed to be in here without me, and certainly shouldn't be touching my—"

I stop when I reach the entryway to the living room, blocked off by a purple foil partition that reaches the floor. Holding the foil in place is a cardboard bat, cute and not creepy. I part the foil with two hands, like a curtain.

Immediately I am hit by the smell of fog juice and something else I can't quite place.

On the coffee table, the lights of Spookyville are aglow, there's a pillow of fog enshrouding the town. I'd always imagined the town as existing somewhere in the middle of the country, a less humid climate, but now it looks like a New England fishing town.

As my eyes adjust to the darkness, I can see that there's the outline of a body sitting on the couch. Its back is straight, small feet perched over the edge.

"Cecily," I say, nearly yelling her name now, looking for a

response.

"I'm sorry," her voice comes from behind me, not from the couch. I turn to see that Cecily's standing in the spare room's doorway. "Don't be mad, Miss Maggie. I wanted to surprise you. Set things up a little earlier this year."

My heart melts a little that she wants to do something for me.

And then I remember the body on the couch and a chill washes over me.

I used to have a posable latex skeleton. It was about the size of a small child, but I had to throw it out last year after Cecily twisted his arm a little too vigorously and forced part of his sharp wire armature out of his shoulder.

The shape on the couch is too big to be the latex skeleton, anyway.

I *could* flip on the overhead light and instantly reveal what Cecily's set up on the couch, but I don't have the strength. Instead I cross to the couch to get a better look, bumping my knee against the coffee table and sending Spookyville rattling.

There are two of them seated there, not one.

Brian is slouching, the flesh and musculature of his neck too moldered to sit up straight.

Beside him, Jill is looking considerably better, if it weren't for the blackened tips of her fingers she would just look hungry. Her eyes are sunken dried slits and her lips shriveled, but otherwise she looks alive.

Cecily has opened the blue boxes, the coffins, even though she promised me that she wouldn't snoop.

I wonder how long she's known that the containers didn't hold something boring like old clothes.

"They don't scare me," Cecily says. "They're smelly but they don't scare me. I think they're neat."

Yesterday, I wondered if Cecily's precociousness, the fact that she has a cell phone and is interested in more modern horror fare, was going to stop her from wanting to be around me. An old fuddy-duddy.

Looking at the small bodies on the couch, their desiccated faces and putrid bellies, I get the feeling.

And it's the strongest the feeling has been in a long time. Maybe even since I was Cecily's age.

"What did you do with Heather?" I ask, looking around. She was the oldest of the three, she made it the farthest. Heather was thirteen and a half before I boxed her up.

"She was too heavy. Can you help me?" Cecily has crept up behind me while my back was turned. Her fingers close around my hand and the human contact surprises me. We hold hands while on the CD a thunder crack echoes through a cemetery.

"Yes, I can help you." I say, glad that the season has started early and that I have someone to share it with.

At least for a little longer.

AUTHOR'S NOTE

Zero Lives Remaining was originally released as a limited edition hardcover. Although that's not the version you currently hold in your hands, I feel that the editors, filmmakers, and artists who helped make that edition so special are still deserving of mention and thanks: Ken Wood, Sarah Wood, John Boden, Nick Gucker, Frank Walls, Yannick Bouchard, and Mike Lombardo of Reel Splatter Productions (who made an astonishing live-action trailer for the book, which you can watch online)

And a special thanks to Tod Clark, Alexander "Cold Fire" Boden, David Brady, Erik Myrnes, Dylan S-C, and Kaleigh Brodbeck.

"Starting Early" originally appeared in *Dark Hallows*, a collection of Halloween stories edited by Mark Parker. Big thanks to Mark for commissioning the story.

ADAM CESARE is a New Yorker who lives in Philadelphia.

His work has been featured in numerous magazines and anthologies. His nonfiction has appeared in *Paracinema, The LA Review of Books* and other venues. He also writes a (sometimes) monthly column about the intersection of horror fiction and film for *Cemetery Dance Online* and produces a weekly YouTube review show called *Project: Black T-Shirt*.

His novels and novellas are available in ebook and paperback from Amazon, Barnes & Noble, and all other fine retailers.

Please visit www.adamcesare.com to learn more.

Author photo by John Urbancik.

Download a FREE exclusive ebook by visiting Adamcesare.com.

The Blackest Eyes is a mini collection of two short stories. The title story is cautionary tale about keeping sharks in captivity. This ebook is free for everyone who signs up for *Adam Cesare's Mailing List of Terror*.

What are you waiting for? Go to adamcesare.com and sign up today!

Want more Cesare? Read on to get your fix!

PRAISE FOR *THE CON SEASON*

"If what you're looking for is an exciting, gory romp through the familiar stomping grounds of slasher/survival horror, this book provides that in ample quantity with a joie de mort rivaling the best 80's slasher. At the same time, it is a fairly *cutting* view of the relationships between creator, performer, and fan. Adam Cesare does not disappoint! Buy this book!" —**Bracken MacLeod**, author of *Stranded*

"*The Con Season* is a lean and mean novel. It pulls no punches. Filled with interesting characters and some truly thrilling sequences, this is a novel that everyone should immediately go out and download." —The Fiction and Film Emporium

This novella is available in ebook, audiobook, and paperback.

Horror movie starlet Clarissa Lee is beautiful, internationally known, and…completely broke.

To cap off years of questionable financial and personal decisions, Clarissa accepts an invitation to participate in a "fully immersive" fan convention. She arrives at an off-season summer camp and finds what was supposed to be a quick buck has become a real-life slasher movie.

Deep in the woods of Kentucky with a supporting cast of B-level celebrities, Clarissa must fight to survive the deadly game that the con's organizers have rigged against her.

A demented, funny, bloody, and strangely-poignant horror novel.

PRAISE FOR *TRIBESMEN*

"Sick and sardonic and just plain brilliant." —Duane Swierczynski, author of *Fun & Games* and *Canary*

"The best new writer I've read in years. Wonderfully lean prose and edge-of-your-seat thrills. Drop everything else and start reading *Tribesmen*." —Nate Kenyon, author of *Day One* and *Sparrow Rock*

"A cunning, cinematic redmeat feast for weird film lovers and horror freaks, Adam Cesare's *Tribesmen* is a first-rate literary midnight movie, and a blistering debut. BRING YOUR FRIENDS!" —John Skipp

"*Tribesmen* is a gory and clever homage to those Italian cannibal flicks that we all love so dearly, but without the real-life animal cruelty! Highly recommended." -Jeff Strand, author of *Pressure* and *Wolf Hunt*.

"Sometimes everything goes wrong, in the best possible way. Think *Snuff* and *Cannibal Holocaust* meeting at a midnight movie. And then give one of them a camera, the other a knife." – Stephen Graham Jones, author of *It Came from Del Rio*, *The Gospel of Z* and *Demon Theory*

This novella is available in ebook, audiobook, and paperback.

DON'T FUCK WITH THE NATIVES!

Thirty years ago, cynical sleazeball director Tito Bronze took a tiny cast and crew to a desolate island. His goal: to exploit the local tribes, spray some guts around, cash in on the gore-spattered 80s Italian cannibal craze.

But the pissed-off spirits of the island had other ideas. And before long, guts were squirting behind the scenes, as well. While the camera kept rolling...

Tribesmen is Adam Cesare's blistering tribute to *Cannibal Holocaust* and Lucio Fulci: a no-bullshit glimpse into grindhouse filmmaking, stuffed inside a rocket of tropical non-stop mayhem.

PRAISE FOR *VIDEO NIGHT*

"Hit that first chapter. It'll hook you, and the next time you look up, you'll have swallowed the book. It'll be nesting inside you like a seed, like an egg, like an invasion." —**Stephen Graham Jones**, author of *Mongrels*

"If you put together the gore, action, monsters, and sense of excitement that made '80s horror movies so great, you'll only have about half of what makes *Video Night* a must-read tome for horror fans." —***Horrortalk***

"The momentum keeps building. The stakes keep escalating. The monsters just keep getting worse and worse, the catastrophic mayhem more juicy and hopeless. Best of all, the writing moves like a greased torpedo, compulsively readable as it rockets through your brain [...] Adam Cesare's gonna be a Fango superstar." —***Fangoria***

"*Video Night* is a sharp, smart, energetic novel which pays tribute to all the brilliantly gross horror comedies of the VHS era, even as it carves out its own corners of shock literature." —***Daily Grindhouse***

This novel is available in ebook and paperback.

Who better to repel a body-snatching alien invasion than a group of teenage horror nerds?

Billy and Tom are best friends, but each knows that at the end of the school year they'll be moving in different directions. But why not go out with a bang and throw one last video night? They can invite some girls over, order a pizza, then maybe try and fight the alien infection that's taken hold over their suburban town.

It's *The Breakfast Club* meets *The Night of the Creeps* in this slime-drenched '80s horror romp.

PRAISE FOR *MERCY HOUSE*

"Adam Cesare's *Mercy House* is a rowdy, gory, blood-soaked horror tale guaranteed to keep you up at night. And if that was all it was, I'd have been a happy reader. But Cesare has a maturity far and away beyond his years. His characters are treated with a surprising capacity for understanding and empathy, giving them an unexpected depth rarely seen among the nightmare crowd. *Mercy House* is the kind of novel you sprint through, eating up the pages as fast as you can turn them, and yet it lingers in the mind like a haunting memory, or the ghost of a smell. Cesare is poised to take the reins of the new generation. Looking for the new face of horror? This is it right here." —**Joe McKinney**, Bram Stoker Award–winning author of *The Dead Won't Die* and *Dead City*

"*Mercy House* is 100% distilled nightmare juice. Adam Cesare notches up the horror to nigh-unbearable levels. Even my skin was screaming by the end of this book." —**Nick Cutter**, author of *The Troop*

"Adam Cesare makes his presence felt with *Mercy House*. A no-holds-barred combo of survival horror and the occult." — **Laird Barron**, author of *The Beautiful Thing That Awaits Us All*

"This is extreme horror at its best, so don't step into this book with an uneasy stomach. You must wait sixty minutes after eating before opening up *Mercy House*."—*LitReactor*

This novel is available as an ebook from Random House Hydra.

Welcome to Mercy House, a state-of-the-art retirement home that appears perfectly crisp, clean, and orderly...but nothing could be farther from the truth. In Adam Cesare's thrilling novel, the residents will find little mercy—only a shocking eruption of unfathomable horror.

PRAISE FOR *THE FIRST ONE YOU EXPECT*

"*The First One You Expect* is a fast, sexy, fun, dangerous read, and enough of a taste to make me hope Cesare ventures into crime fiction regularly." —**Spinetingler Magazine**

"With *The First One You Expect*, Cesare yet again shows not only his passion and knowledge of the ins and outs of the genre, but he is able to turn it into a riveting and original story that holds a bit of a mirror up to many of us horror fiends." —**HorrorNewsNet**

This novella is available in ebook and paperback.

When he's not holding down a dead-end job or lurking in his mother's basement, Tony Anastos spends his time shooting ultra-low-budget horror flicks.

After meeting his sexy fame-hungry coworker Anna, he sees an opportunity to launch his career into cult stardom. But when Tony's plan to jolt their next film's Kickstarter into overdrive calls for real blood, he will sacrifice the last bit of his humanity for a shot at recognition.

But it makes sense. Look at him. The stuff he makes, I mean, he's the first one you expect.

PRAISE FOR *EXPONENTIAL*

"*Exponential* is fast-paced fun, a rollicking monster movie in 200 quick-moving pages." —*Ain'tItCool*

"*Exponential* is an excellent novel, one of the best creature features I've read in years, and will very likely appear on my Top 10 Horror Reads of 2014..." —*Horror After Dark*

"...Adam Cesare's mix of grim violence and old school horror movie references make for a great read." —*Rue Morgue #152*

Pick up this novel in ebook or paperback.

Can anything stop a creature that won't stop growing?

Sam Taylor just wants a friend. Is that too much to ask? His only mistake is finding that friend in Felix, a lab mouse that Sam rescues from the top-secret facility where he works as a janitor. Shortly after his rescue, the mouse begins to change, to swell. There's something new growing underneath Felix's fur. Growing very fast.

Holed up in a roadside bar, four survivors—a woman who's lost everything, her drug dealer, a tribal police officer, and a professional gambler—are all that stand between the rampaging beast and the city of Las Vegas. But as the monster keeps growing—and eating—how long until it's able to topple the walls protecting them?

PRAISE FOR *THE SUMMER JOB*

"The prologue of *The Summer Job* is one the best and scariest openings to a horror novel I've ever read. […] The rest of the novel is equally great. It's a little like Jack Ketchum's *Offseason*, if you replace the cannibalistic savages with a satanic cult, but I feel so strongly about *The Summer Job* that I'll go out on a limb and say that I believe it's better than *Offseason*. I really do." —*LitReactor*

"The textbook definition of a nail-biter. *The Summer Job* is a kissing cousin to inbred classics from masters like Ketchum and Kilborn. Cesare's best novel yet." —**Bloody Disgusting**

"Cesare's latest is a knockout…There's a potent retro vibe running through Cesare's work, in general—he's the closest thing literary horror has to its own Jim Mickle or Ti West." —**Complex**

Check out this novel in ebook and paperback.

Massive nights, picturesque days: there is nothing Claire doesn't love about her summer job in Mission, Massachusetts. Claire is just trying to keep her head down and start a new life after burning out in the city, but those kids out in the woods seem like they throw awesome ragers...

It's only once she's in too deep that Claire discovers the real tourist trade that keeps the town afloat, it's then that her soul-searching in Mission becomes a fight for her life.

Crazed parties, dark rituals, and unexpected betrayals abound in this modern folk horror novel from the author of *The Con Season* and *Video Night*.

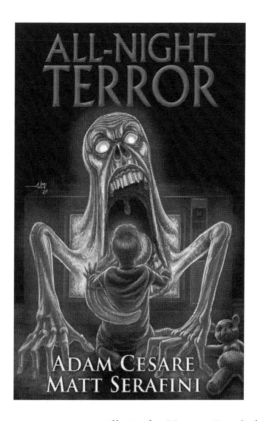

You're invited to experience *All Night Terror*. Don't look for help, your weaker friends will be too scared to attend, but you're in for the nightmare of your life.

Sit down in front of the TV and prepare for a late-night odyssey of wicked shocks as a horror movie marathon becomes a bloodbath before your very eyes. It starts when a disgruntled cable host seizes control of a television station, determined to give his viewers an evening they won't soon forget. One where monsters of all shapes and sizes rise up against mankind. One where deranged killers prowl the night for a variety of victims. And one where cinema itself haunts its creators and creations.

Join modern horror stars Adam Cesare (*Tribesmen*, *Zero Lives Remaining*) and Matt Serafini (*Feral*, *Island Red*) as they bring you ten tales of fear that will have you shivering between the pages.

All Night Terror—good to the last slash.

For more titles and news about upcoming work be sure to visit AdamCesare.com to sign up for the mailing list or find Adam on Amazon.

Made in the USA
Middletown, DE
14 February 2017